GENERATIONS

The Pressure of Change

Anne Mason

A Family of Millwrights:

Disinherited
A Measure of Happiness
Generations

1

In the moment before the horse's hooves hit the ground, it was silent and still, like a photograph. Then someone screamed: blood was spurting from the back of a man's head as he crumpled to the ground. Those around him knew him and they lifted his corpse, for that's what it was. He had died, instantly.

The millwrights' yard was busy and noisy with the sound of tools as the men bent to their tasks. The door to the yard opened with a bang and the men looked up to see who was coming in in such a hurry. Those who carried James Spandler came from the door, down the passage under the first-floor rooms, to the yard. They rounded the corner and, as they appeared, the men frowned. Then a young man with a disfigured face sprang forward.

'Pa!' he cried. Robert came out of the cottage to see what was happening. He pointed to one of the men.

'Fetch the doctor!' The man left but when Robert stepped nearer he knew that the doctor would have a wasted journey. He did not send for Hannah. Instead, keeping his voice as level as he could, he thanked those who had carried him and asked if they would move him into the store room. Then he turned to a group of men.

'Measure him and start work on the coffin.'

'No, Robert, we'll do it.' Another young man stood next to the man with the disfigured face. 'We'll do it,' he repeated. Robert looked from one to the other of James Spandler's sons. Jim, James' eldest son, continued, 'but first we will go to Ma, before she hears from someone else.' Robert nodded.

'Go now because the news will travel quickly,' he said, 'it always does.' He put his hand to his forehead and rubbed it. James Spandler had been his younger brother.

In the doorway of a large cottage another young man was lolling against the door frame. He smiled to himself as he turned and went back indoors.

The bell tolled and trading at the market stopped. As men removed their hats the crowd fell silent: a senior member of the Spandler family was being taken to his final resting place.

The procession made its way from their millwrights' yard, past the King's Arms and along the railings at the west side of St Nicholas's graveyard. A young man in the family drew the eyes of the crowd: such was his size that he lolled from one leg to the other as he walked causing his whole body to quiver, the effort making his face red and shiny. He turned and, catching the eye of a man who was behind him, he smirked. His cousin ignored him. However many in the crowd had noticed and people frowned, pursed their lips and looked at each other.

After the committal the family returned to the yard, to the home of Robert and Mary Spandler. He was the master-in-charge and it was his privilege to live in the cottage there. As head of the family he provided a meal for everyone.

Many people were talking to Hannah, the widow, but Henry looked for the sons, James and Frederick; he would speak with his aunt later. When they were younger, the brothers had been apprentices at the yard and Henry had been given charge of their learning. He was very fond of them. He rested an arm on each and looked at James.

'Jim, you are now the man at the head your family,' Henry spoke slowly and deliberately, 'and I understand.' He turned to the other young man. 'Freddie, I know that you will support him.' They both nodded, knowing why their cousin understood.

'But, the yard, Henry, the yard – Father's death will affect more than us.' Jim's eyes flicked from his cousin to his brother as his grief altered his voice.

'I know,' Henry sighed, 'Uncle Robert has not done what he said he would – sell his share to your father – and now it is too late. That would have made you the master and left out Edmund.' They were quiet for a few moments. Each of them looked across to the other side of the yard where Edmund sat, steadily eating his way through a huge plate of food. Henry continued, 'Do you know he turned and smirked at me during the procession?' Jim and Freddie both scowled which made the scars on Freddie's face move. This would make people who didn't know him smile but Henry and James were used to Freddie's odd faces: as an infant a coal from the fire had badly burnt him and taken his right eye.

'I know that when you told me of the plan that you, my father and Uncle Robert had thought up, the idea that I would be master-in-charge was daunting,' said Jim, 'but, then, it wouldn't have been until I was a lot older and more experienced in the business.'

'But even now you would do better than that oaf,' suggested Freddie.

'Pa's death is sad for us,' Jim stopped and swallowed, 'but for the business it's the worst thing that could happen.'

'We can only wait and see,' suggested Henry, 'although I think that Robert is going to miss your father. They've been together since they were apprentices.'

'As he misses your father as well,' replied Jim. Henry drew a deep breath before he spoke.

'Yes, grandfather started handing over the running of his yard to them while he was still alive and the three brothers did everything between them when I was first an apprentice.' He paused. 'That was until my father had his foolish notion of making his fortune in London. It would be so different if he was here now,' he shrugged, 'but he isn't.' They stopped talking and stared at the ground.

'Do you remember when you discussed it with them? Did you not tell us afterwards that there was something said about young Richard?' asked Jim, who was the millwright overseeing Richard's apprenticeship. 'He's a good lad, nothing like his older brother – he's only thirteen yet but he'll make a millwright.' He spoke with confidence, but Henry was shaking his head.

'I think the problem with that will be their mother. With your father at his side Robert was stronger. However, Aunt Mary favours Edmund and would not like the idea that Robert would change his will so that Richard becomes master-in-charge on his death instead of Edmund, even if they are both her sons.'

'But Edmund is incapable!' blurted Jim.

'She will say that he has done his apprenticeship twice,' continued Henry. 'It is seventeen years since he started at the yard. You know that Robert and Edmund have spent most evenings in the workroom since that discussion?' They nodded.

'I remember last year when he had to sit with the apprentices and make a cog wheel again.' Freddie's one eye showed his amusement.

'Yes, but I cannot see any improvement,' insisted Jim, 'and I fear that with Pa gone the learning will stop. Ed doesn't like it – only last month I was working late and Robert was trying to insist he went to the workroom whilst he sat on the bench outside the cottage with a pout on his face like a girl and his mother stood behind him telling Robert Ed needed to come inside for something to eat before he did any more work!'

'As if he would fade away to nothing!' Freddie's look of scorn moved the scar that covered the socket where his eye had been and this time there was a flash of amusement on the others' faces.

'We can only wait and see,' repeated Henry, 'but certainly I cannot approach Robert about it at the moment. Let's see how Ed is – perhaps the realisation that his father is now on his own at the head of this business,' Henry paused and shrugged, 'well it might make him start to apply himself to the craft.' He looked up to see them shaking their heads.

'You're starting to sound like Uncle Robert,' said James.

'Ed is more likely to stop making any effort at all because he knows the yard will be his now, whatever he does,' added Freddie.

'Well, it seems that we'll need to work all the harder to compensate for him then,' Henry's eyes flicked between their faces, 'because it's either that or stand and watch grandfather's yard become nothing.'

'At least we'll have this young man to help us,' said Freddie as Henry's brother Thomas approached.

'Help with what?' he asked, his eyes moving between the three men.

'With stopping Ed from destroying the yard when he is charge.'

'It may not happen,' Thomas nodded his head towards Edmund, 'because he may eat himself to death before then. Besides, at the moment, I think we need to worry more about how we're going to manage without your father.'

'Yes,' agreed Henry, 'it is going to be difficult but we have to succeed.' He turned and his wife Mary-Ann, surrounded by their children, came into his line of sight. His frown deepened. Mary-Ann was becoming large and he could see that it was nearing time for the baby to be born.

A few days later he borrowed the cart from the yard together with the horse, which they shared with the King's Arms next door, and went and brought Abigail, Mary-Ann's mother, from the farm near Caister where she lived. She looked after the women in the village when they birthed so each time she had come to help Mary-Ann. Last time, when William was born, both Mary-Ann and the baby had nearly died. Now that she was about to give birth again Henry kept himself busy at the yard and Thomas, who lived with them, arranged with Robert that he could stay at the cottage when the birth began. When they returned to Francis Buildings each evening they found the two women happy and unconcerned. Henry was perplexed: after the difficulties Mary-Ann had had last time he expected them to be as tense as he was. Abigail explained that the baby was the right way up to be born easily but Henry shook his head. The complexities of the millwrights' craft he understood but the things of women bewildered him.

It was the third week in August, ten days after Abigail had arrived, when Henry saw her going up to their bedroom with fresh straw. He knew what that meant: she was protecting their bed from soiling as the baby was born. Abigail seemed to want him and Thomas to go so he kissed his wife quickly and they left for the yard.

'The baby's started to come,' said Henry to Robert when they arrived.

'So I'll need to stay with you tonight,' added Thomas. Robert nodded.

'I hope it's alright,' he said, looking with concern at Henry.

'Abigail seems happy, which is different to last time,' replied Henry, 'so I hope that means it'll be easier for Mary-Ann. What work is there that will leave me with no time to think about it?' Robert gave a short laugh.

'I'm pleased you said that. Edmund woke up this morning wheezing louder than Bessie. I was going to send him out to see if he could supervise the two new apprentices while they try and assess the work Bart's mill needs. He wants to take out a contract with us.'

'Really? He always said he never would but then, after the trouble he had in the storms last winter...' Henry shrugged but then continued, 'I know it'll take a lot to bring it up to where we'd take it on – the last time I was in there, there was more wrong with it than right.'

'Which is why I said the new apprentices should look at it.'

'And you put Ed in charge,' suggested Henry, 'because there'll be so much needing doing even he would see it.' Robert frowned. Henry gave a small smile and looked directly at him before continuing, 'I'm only saying how it is.'

'I know,' Robert sighed. 'But for today you can enjoy being out there with the younger ones and they'll learn a lot from being with you.' Henry grinned.

'And it should be enough to take my mind off what is happening at home – but send a runner if a message comes.'

On his way out, Henry checked Bessie's dials and Freddie nodded at him.

'She is running well today,' he told him.

'I know and I'm sure she's well looked after but I like to see.' Freddie, and some of the other men who had heard, laughed. Henry had been the first millwright at the yard who could control Bessie, the stationary steam engine that powered the tools and, even though there were others who could do it now, they knew that he would always check.

Later, out at Bart's mill, they had stopped for midday bread when Henry noticed a young boy running towards them. His mouth went dry and he coughed as he tried to swallow.

'M-Mr S-Spandler, s-sir,' panted the boy. He was smiling and Henry let out the breath he had been holding. 'You have a new son!' The two apprentices cheered but Henry frowned at the boy. 'Oh, and Mrs Spandler is well.' At last Henry grinned and patted the boy on the back. Although he was sure that Robert would have paid him before he left he gave him a penny and the boy ran off.

When Henry returned to the yard Thomas was still working at one of the lathes, so he busied himself tidying up. Thomas looked up at him.

'I thought you'd be getting away as quickly as possible tonight.'

'I'm waiting for you.'

'But I thought I was staying here.'

'There's no need now that it's all over. Come on, call in at the cottage and tell Mary that you're coming home with me.'

'B-But…'

'Do you not want to see my new son?'

Thomas grinned. 'Yes of course. I just thought that you'd want some time with your family tonight.'

'You're my family, remember? And besides which Mary-Ann said this morning that you're to come and see him as soon as possible.'

'I don't understand. Why?'

Henry smiled. 'You'll see.'

The two men strode along North Road to Francis Buildings without speaking. They did, however, keep glancing at each other, grinning, and increasing their speed so that by the time they arrived they were breathless. They burst through the front door, panting heavily, and quickly entered the living room.

'Pa! Uncle Tom!' The children shouted, causing Abigail to put her head through the door from the kitchen

'Shh! Yer Ma may be sleeping.' She turned to the men as Henry went around and ruffled each child's hair. 'Go up and see.' Thomas glanced up to where the bedroom was and hesitated.

'Come on,' said Henry as he shifted his weight from one foot to another, 'she said you were to come with me.' Thomas shook his head as he followed Henry back out of the living room, into the passage and up the stairs: Henry usually spent time with Mary-Ann on his own when the children were new-born. They reached the top of the stairs and went through the children's room into Henry and Mary-Ann's. She was awake and smiled at them as they entered. Henry crossed the room. He looked down at her in the bed for a few moments while he stroked her cheek.

'It's never easy but that was better than William's,' she said, looking towards the baby in the cradle next to her bed. Henry leaned over and picked him up. His eyes skimmed over his face and he kissed his forehead. Then he looked at Mary-Ann and smiled. She nodded and he turned to Thomas who was hesitating by the door.

'Thomas, meet your newest nephew,' he paused, his eyes on his brother's face, 'Thomas Spandler.' Thomas's mouth opened. He crossed the room in two steps and took the baby whom Henry held out. For a moment he concentrated on controlling his clumsiness as he made his hold of the child more comfortable. Then he looked at Henry and Mary-Ann, his face beaming.

'You mean, you're calling him after me!'

'Yes,' Henry laughed, 'and our grandfather! Now you see why we wanted you to be here.' Thomas looked from Henry to Mary-Ann and back to the baby.

'We'll have to call him Tom or you'll be sending me up to bed instead of him!' They all laughed. 'Thank you – I'm so happy.'

2

When Robert first became master-in-charge one of the changes he made was to provide the men with tea in the mornings: some of the men would have come in from early jobs and he remembered being so cold when he arrived that he was clumsy and unable to think straight, so he knew that allowing them to spend a while standing around Bessie warming themselves was not a waste of time. Whilst the men drank their tea Robert and James would talk together, sometimes pointing at some of their workers, before Robert announced their tasks for the day. Now, with James dead, Robert sought out Henry in the mornings and most evenings after work finished for the day they could be found in the King's Arms discussing the following day's business over a tankard of ale. In the months following James's death everyone at the yard could see who was replacing him.

'Henry I'm going to start bringing Edmund to these meetings,' said Robert one evening in early September.' Henry nodded.

'I think it would be a good idea,' replied Henry. 'Ed needs to take on some of the running of the yard now, like grandfather did with you. Mary-Ann will be pleased when I start coming straight home at the end of the day.' Robert's eyes opened wide.

'No, I didn't mean he would replace you,' he croaked, 'just that he would join us. I need you here as well.'

'I see – but don't expect me to agree with him just because he's your son.'

'I'd be disappointed if you did!' They both laughed. 'I'm bringing him because he and his mother keep asking – but he needs to begin to realise how little he actually understands.' They stopped talking until Henry suddenly broke the silence.

'What do you think is the future for Spandler's yard?' His voice was clipped. Robert's eyes dropped to the floor and his shoulders slumped. In softer tones Henry continued, 'you do not have to do what they say.'

'But she is so insistent. She brought money into this business which is why my father wanted me to marry her – so she says her son should benefit from it.'

'But she married you, Robert – and that money is yours now. She would squander it by pandering to her lazy son which is why the law gives you charge over it. She is a woman and, as Edmund's mother, cannot see his failings. Grandfather wanted you to marry her to improve the yard, not to destroy it.'

'Edmund is my son as well,' said Robert without meeting Henry's eyes.

'Yes, but don't you be blind to him like his Ma! Have him here as we discuss the business. I'll try to help him to become someone who could follow you as master-in-charge – but I won't just let him have his own way.' Robert nodded. Henry grinned as he continued, 'so he will be with us in the morning?' Robert smiled but raised his eyebrows: everyone knew that Edmund didn't roll out of the cottage door until after everyone else had started working.

The following evening Henry went to the King's Arms. He was followed ten minutes later by Robert who was alone.

'Edmund will be along in a moment. I've just had an argument with him and Mary – they wanted us to have it later.'

'You mean after Ed had eaten?'

'I told them that this was part of the working day, so it must happen as soon as the yard stops for the evening.' The door opened. 'Here he is now.' They picked up their tankards of ale and moved to one of the booths.

Edmund joined them for the next three evenings but on the fourth he said he was unwell and went to the cottage. Over the following few weeks he was sometimes there but in the end he stopped coming altogether.

'No Ed again tonight?' asked Henry the first time he'd been absent all week.

'No, I don't think we'll see him very often.'

'He'll come if he thinks there's some big decision to be made which he wants to be part of,' suggested Henry, 'but other than that he is not interested in running the yard.'

'They're still saying we should have it later.'

'Edmund and his Ma – and I suppose they say you're favouring me?' Robert nodded.

'Yes – do you know last night Mary suggested we did it whilst we ate? I think it is so that she can be there and agree with everything Edmund says.' The two men looked at each other and Henry smiled.

'I wouldn't want to come between you and Mary. Perhaps if I say I don't want to join you?' Robert's eyes widened.

'You won't though, will you?' he said. Henry's eyes twinkled with amusement and Robert relaxed and returned his smile.

'It was my grandfather's yard and'– Henry's smile vanished – 'although my father did not value it, I do. I will do all I can to maintain it.'

'Would that your father had died before he sold his share so that you would become master-in-charge after me.' Henry nodded as Robert continued, 'I would enjoy this time, us both working together to improve the yard. As it is I....' Robert stopped and stared into his ale for a few moments before lifting it to his mouth and drinking without revealing what he was about to say.

On the twenty-third of December, when work finished for the day at Spandler's yard, the apprentices decorated the yard with greenery which they had collected from the river banks and the area between the town and the sea, known as the Denes. By the time they returned tables had been laid with food, provided by Robert and Mary. The barrel of ale, which had been standing in the corner of the yard for two weeks having been rolled through from the King's Arms, had been unstopped and a tap inserted. The workers at the yard spent the evening in each other's company. As he walked home Henry realised that he had not spent any time with James and Freddie, but he thought no more about it: he would have time to catch up with them at the family celebration the following evening. When he reached Francis Buildings and opened the front door he was enveloped by a sweet, spicy smell and knew what his family's contribution to the feast tomorrow was going to be: Mary-Ann had been baking. She was proud of the tiny oven next to the grate which Henry had put in the back room when they first took on the rent of the whole house. When he went through to the kitchen and saw the biscuits standing cooling in rows he knew that it must have taken her most of the day. He could see that some were plain and others had currants in them. He leant over to have a closer smell and – yes – there were also gingers, his favourite. His family seemed noisier than usual and he realised that they were excited. He smiled to himself: Spandler's yard would be closed for the next three days so he would have plenty of time to spend with them. He drew in a deep breath and let it out with a sigh. He had memories of Christmases when his life was sad and, although he tried, he could not forget. He could hear his family in the adjoining room and the present gave him strength: he shook himself and dispelled the memories.

That night in bed Henry and Mary-Ann snuggled together, enjoying each other's warmth. In the darkness his hand found her face and he drew one of his fingers down from her forehead, along her nose and onto her lips before kissing her gently. His hands slipped inside her nightgown, which was open at the top in readiness for feeding Tom, and he cupped her breasts.

'I'm expecting my bleeding soon so if you came to me it would be unlikely to start another baby,' she whispered in his ear, wriggling with anticipation as she did so. In the darkness Henry smiled.

'If you're sure. I don't want you to carry another child – I am happy with those you have given me.'

'No Henry, I cannot be sure. No-one can – but my mother says just before the bleeding is the best time because the blood would wash your seed away.'

'I'd struggle if I lost you,' he said.

'And I struggle if I lost you – climbing out on mill-caps and other dangerous things. Look at what happened to Uncle James. None of us can be sure Henry, so why stop ourselves? Besides I bore Tom without too much weakness afterwards.'

'But William…?'

'I was unlucky, he grew awkwardly inside me. If I'm unlucky again, well,' she paused, 'I'm not going to think about it – weather that storm if it arrives – but for now...' She reached up to his head and pulled it towards her. Her lips found his and they stopped talking.

The following afternoon Henry's family walked up to the yard from Francis Buildings. Five-year-old Harry walked with his Uncle Thomas at the front, followed by Carrie and Louisa with three-year-old William between them. Henry carried his youngest son, Tom, and Mary-Ann held Henry's arm. Henry was happy. The sound of their steps changed as they walked on the wooden planks that covered the town drain that went under the road. Henry looked across the road to where the drain flowed down Garrison Walk on its way to the riverside where its noxious contents were shovelled onto boats to be taken to farms along the river. Henry had grown up in Garrison Walk. He could recall the sadness of that time after his father sold his share of the yard, went to London and was robbed of all his money. He'd returned poor and ill. Henry, with his older sisters Eliza and Mary, had struggled to raise the family and many of his younger siblings had died. His life was so different now: his own family gave him happiness which offset the fact that he would no longer inherit a share of the yard and become master-in-charge – and he'd dreamt that one of his daughters would marry above herself. He smiled as Harry held his nose and protested at the smell.

They arrived at the hall and the children went into a roped-off area where Rachel, Henry's sister, had charge of them. Mary-Ann took the bowls of biscuits from her basket and put them with the other food on the long table in front of the cottage. Henry stood and looked around him at his extended family. He noticed a young woman standing next to Freddie and realised that this must be Ruth: Freddie had told him about the arrangement that his father had made before his death. Uncle James had done well for his second son and he wondered to himself why Jim had not been matched with her but he was standing next to Freddie smiling at them both, so he was happy with the arrangement. She was a beautiful young woman, distinctive because of her bright red hair. As Henry approached them Freddie beamed and Henry could understand his happiness: with his disfigurement he was very fortunate that her father had agreed that she should marry him.

'Henry this is Ruth. We are to be married on Friday.' Henry bowed slightly towards her. 'My mother's brother, in London, he knows Ruth's father.' Henry nodded in understanding.

'So, you are a Londoner,' he stated.

'I am,' she smiled as she responded which caused her nose to wrinkle, 'my father is over there talking to my aunt.' Henry followed her eyes and could clearly see that the man standing next to Hannah was her brother. Without thinking his eyes flicked between him and the top of Ruth's head. Ruth laughed and continued, 'It was my mother who had the red hair. She died when my youngest brother was born.' Henry's face turned red. While he was talking to Ruth he was aware that Freddie and Jim were looking at each other and then at himself.

'Henry, can you just come over here with me,' said Jim, 'there's something I need to speak with you about.' Henry frowned because it seemed another rudeness in front of Ruth to add to his own but moved away with Jim.

'What is it?'

'It's something we need to tell you before Ma makes her announcement.'

'What announcement?' Henry was concerned now because Jim was perspiring and his eyes were moving rapidly between his mother and his brother. 'What do you mean?'

'Ma's going to move to London, to be near her brother.' Jim stopped and drew a deep breath. 'Freddie and I are going with her.' Henry did not speak. His head felt as if it was expanding and contracting as he struggled to assimilate Jim's words. When he did speak it was quietly and this took Jim by surprise. He had been prepared for Henry to shout but he had to move nearer to hear him.

'Why? The yard?' Henry exuded the words through his teeth. 'What will we do? It will die without your share – there's not enough work!' Henry bared his teeth and his eyes flashed between Jim and his brother Freddie.

'We do not intend to sell our share. Our uncle in London says there is enough work there to support us.'

'B-B-But your skills...' Henry's voice faltered.

'You know we have trained others,' said Jim. Henry nodded: he and Robert had discussed how they could use two of the apprentices who had almost finished their training.

'Yes,' he replied with a sigh. 'We had thought that we'd have to send them off to seek work elsewhere. This way we can retain them – but I would have preferred to have kept you two and let them go. Now the only Spandlers in the yard will be Robert, myself, Thomas and Ed – oh and young Richard of course.'

'Sorry,' Jim was shaking his head, 'but Richard is thinking of coming with us as well – but we will be coming back.'

Henry shrugged. 'Perhaps, but perhaps not. You'll have children and settle your family there – and Ruth won't want to leave her family to come and live here. But I wish you well – even if you're leaving us with just Ed for company.' He nodded to the other side of the yard where Ed was looking at them and smirking. 'I think he already knows.'

Henry stayed for the rest of the celebration although he felt like running away and leaving it. For a moment he imagined himself going down to the docks and finding work on a boat that would take him far away but when he wandered over to a roped-off area where his children were playing he knew that he could never leave them.

Robert stood on one of the benches and everyone went quiet.

'Another Christmas is here. It is good to see us all joined together again.' He smiled as his eyes passed over everyone. 'I was sad last night, realising that my brother James would not be here this year – but it is good that we have happy times like this. This year Henry and Mary-Ann have again added to the Spandlers and Ruth will be a Spandler by the end of the week. Our lives continue, 'he turned to Hannah, James's widow, 'and some of us will not be here next year.' Henry had been looking at him but as Hannah started to speak he dropped his eyes and looked into his tankard. As she spoke about going to London he felt that some were watching him, and he was glad that Jim had had the wisdom to forewarn him. When she said that Jim and Freddie were going with her, Thomas gasped and turned to Henry but he continued to stare at his ale.

As Henry walked home with his family he remembered how content he'd been when they'd walked the other way a few hours earlier. Now, as he looked at his family ahead of him, he felt an insecurity and sense of foreboding which he recognised from his youth. After the children were asleep Henry, Mary-Ann and Thomas talked into the night as they tried to imagine the way forward. When they finally retired for the night Henry allowed himself the tears he had been controlling since the conversation with Jim that afternoon. Mary-Ann hugged him close to her and, eventually, they drifted into sleep.

3

Two years passed. The winters had been stormy. Spandler's advised the millers to lock their mills down but the competition between them was such that none wanted to be the first to stop. When the wind gusted it could suddenly come from behind a mill, too quickly for the cap to turn: this caused the sails to turn backwards, damaging the cogs. Consequently, there was much work for the yard. Henry still missed Jim and Freddie but the two young apprentices who had become millwrights had stayed at the yard and it had prospered. Edmund rarely met with Henry and Robert, who ran the yard, but he did remind Henry every so often whose inheritance it would be.

Mary-Ann was pregnant again. Henry was worried because she was tired all the time, just as she'd been in William's pregnancy. Rachel, his sister, was going to the house in Francis Building each afternoon and helping Mary-Ann with the children. Mary-Ann said that she was tired only because this was her sixth pregnancy: her Ma had told her once that the first birthing a woman did was often long and sometimes went wrong but after that it was when a woman aged that she found it hard. Mary-Ann kept telling him not to worry but he was still relieved after she was delivered of another girl at the beginning of April.

It was a week after the baby's birth. Henry and his younger brother Thomas, who was by now reaching the end of his apprenticeship, were working at the yard. Earlier that afternoon Henry and Thomas had banked up the furnace to provide the heat which Thomas, who was an iron-moulder, needed to melt the iron. The furnace was a complicated structure, designed to reach high temperatures, and was carefully managed so that the fire never went out. Adjacent to it, and connected by a chamber, was the smaller furnace which heated the boiler to power 'Bessie' the steam engine. The proximity of the smaller furnace meant that, although it was extinguished each evening, it never went completely cold. Each morning fire was moved through the connecting chamber enabling the boiler to be quickly brought up to steam to power the engine which drove many of the tools in the yard. When the larger furnace was at maximum temperature it caused the temperature in Bessie's furnace to rise higher than normal. Robert, Henry's uncle, approached just as Henry was adjusting some of the taps that regulated the flow of steam so that the pressure in the boiler didn't rise too high.

'Another batch of joints?' he asked when Thomas had put down the ladle he'd used to pour molten iron into several moulds.

'Yes,' he replied as he tapped the moulds to release any trapped air bubbles.

Henry turned to Robert. 'I find it amazing how he knows when the iron's been stirred enough.'

'He's learnt his skill well,' Robert commented with a smile at his apprentice. He paused for a moment but then he continued, 'You need to leave those to cool for a while and, while Bess seems to be running well, this is a good time to talk. Come and sit over here.' He led the way to a bench. Henry looked at Thomas and frowned.

When they had sat down Robert looked from one to the other of the two men. 'It's your sister,' he stated.

'Rachel? What's wrong?' Thomas asked. Robert was shaking his head.

The colour drained from Henry's face. 'Eliza? Mary?' The words were strangled; he saw both their faces in his mind although it was nearly ten years since they'd gone to Yorkshire with their husbands.

'Eliza. I've had a letter. You know she was pregnant?' They nodded. 'She bled, and the baby started to come – too early but they couldn't stop it. It was stillborn and Eliza died the following morning. The funeral was today.' As Robert spoke Henry stared directly ahead, his emotions betrayed by the clenching of his fists.

'She used to sing to me at bedtime when mother wasn't well,' murmured Thomas.

'Just you, me, and our sisters Rachel and Mary now,' Henry said to him. He turned back to Robert. 'I expect Mary must know because they live fairly near?'

Robert put an arm on Henry's shoulder. 'She knows. She was there, helping with the birth. You can both have the rest of the afternoon off. Go and see Rachel,' he said as he stood up.

Five minutes later Henry and Thomas arrived at the house of Aunt Hannah, their father's youngest sister. She was a widow and Rachel, their sister, was living with her. Rachel was newly-wed: her husband had moved up to Yorkshire and was staying with his brother, who was married to their sister, Mary, whilst he looked for accommodation. In a few weeks Rachel would join him.

'Eliza gone,' she echoed after Henry told her. She looked at her brothers' faces which were a reflection of her own. 'But I was so looking forward to seeing her again – and the new baby,' she swallowed, 'but now they've both gone.'

'Mary will be there,' offered Thomas as if in compensation.

'I'm so pleased she was with Eliza. At the end I mean,' Rachel explained. 'She wasn't just with in-laws. She had one of us with her.' She was still staring at them.

'It's hard. You going as well,' said Thomas.

'Yes,' added Henry, 'that just leaves us two boys here and you two up there. We must keep in touch.'

Rachel nodded. 'You have your family Henry. I'll really miss the children.' She turned to her younger brother. 'And I'm sure you'll find a woman soon Tom, that is if you haven't already.' He blushed and they all laughed.

'You know your father would be proud of you all,' said Hannah from her chair in the corner, 'especially you young Henry.' Henry nodded, tight lipped.

Rachel put a hand on her elder brother's knee. 'Try not to mind her,' she whispered.

'There's nothing wrong with my hearing, Miss Rachel,' her aunt called out, causing them to smile in spite of the sadness. She turned to Henry. 'Your father never meant for things to turn out the way they did.' Henry looked doubtful but did not speak. 'I'm his sister remember,' she continued, 'just like Rachel is yours. I knew him well. I'm sure he really intended to come back a rich man and you would then have lived the life of a rich man's son.' Henry shrugged. 'He loved you, you know. His intentions were good.'

This was too much for Henry. He stood up. 'I don't believe he went away with the money and spent it all having a wonderful time as some tongues say. He was clearly a broken man when he returned although we didn't talk much.' Here Henry checked himself. She was his aunt, his elder, and he was constrained. He continued more quietly, 'His irresponsibility caused, in some part, the deaths of others of my siblings – and you saw what it did to my mother.'

Hannah nodded, 'Yes it was tragic – and I'm sorry about your sister Eliza – but remember your father would still have been proud of his eldest son. Just like Robert, Elizabeth and I, your father's siblings, are of you, our nephew.'

'Thank-you Aunt Hannah,' he mumbled.

As Henry and Thomas walked back to Francis buildings Thomas said, 'Think that was a bit unexpected, what she said.'

'I know Robert thinks highly of me but I hadn't realised the aunts were watching me. You had problems living with Uncle Robert when you were younger?'

'Yes, but not him – his son really.' Henry looked at him.

'Edmund?' They both nodded. 'I remember now – he was the reason you went to Norwich.'

'He definitely despised me. And did all he could to get me into trouble with his father. Come to think of it, one time when Edmund did something silly his father compared him to you. Said he should be more like his cousin. Ed didn't like that! But I was always in the wrong – he's very much the favoured son.'

'No, I don't like him much. Throws his weight around a bit at the yard – and certainly he has plenty to throw!' They both laughed briefly before Henry continued, 'I'm sure he's one of the reasons Robert went to sea.'

'Robert?'

'His elder brother, Uncle Robert and Aunt Mary's firstborn. Don't you remember when he came back from Middlesex? It was just after you came to us.'

Thomas's frown relaxed. 'Of course. Big man. Bit fumble-fisted?'

'Clumsy, yes, – even you noticed! When Ed started at the yard Robert had already been working for two years. Ed was very clever because, by drawing everyone's attention to Robert, like he did, he hid his own ineptitude. Uncle Robert couldn't see what he was doing, but I think everyone else could. It was Susanna's idea – to leave the yard – after they married. She convinced Robert he wouldn't ever be happy there.'

'Richard didn't have a problem with Edmund,' commented Thomas, 'but then he used to take his side when we fell out.'

'He's so much younger than him that Edmund considers him insignificant. What's more now that Uncle James has died and his sons are going to London and Richard with them it leaves you and me as the only male cousins in the area. He doesn't like us and I know why. Ed considers the yard his. I'm a threat.'

At this point the two men reached the front door: it was unlocked and Henry pushed it open. Mary-Ann, who was sewing whilst she was feeding the baby, looked up surprised.

'You're early,' she said.

Henry nodded. 'Robert let us go.' He dropped into his chair. Mary-Ann looked at his face and knew immediately that something was wrong.

'It's Eliza,' Thomas stated, 'Robert's just told us that she died trying to give birth.' Mary dropped her sewing and her hands flew to her mouth. The baby continued to suck at her breast.

'Our sister Mary was there with her. She bled,' explained Henry. Mary-Ann just nodded. Thomas went through to the kitchen where he moved the kettle onto the heat.

'Do we have tea?' he asked.

'Yes,' replied Mary-Ann, 'here, I'll do it.' She removed the baby from her breast knowing that she was asleep and just sucking for comfort. The baby's tongue and lips continued to move for a few moments but then were still. Henry held out his arms and took her whereupon Mary-Ann followed Thomas to the kitchen. Henry's large, calloused hands were gentle while his eyes moved over the face of his tiny daughter. The hairs in her eyebrows reflected the light; her lips formed a delicate mouth and her chin was small and pointed.

Like Eliza. Eliza! We could call her Eliza! I wonder if Mary-Ann will agree?

Henry's eyes moved from the child and gazed around the room.

This is my home. Most of it I made. The fireplace – he smiled – *was a gift from Uncle Robert.* His eyes rested on the table. *That was the first thing – when we moved in ten years ago. These chairs were from Uncle James; he made them himself for us when we wed. I miss him. Eliza's gone. Strange how you can feel contentment and sadness at the same time.*

He looked again at his daughter. She opened her eyes.

'Hello,' Henry paused, 'Eliza.' The baby's eyes were starting to be able to see properly. The shape she saw was familiar and she was even beginning to realise that it was different to the other similar shape she often saw. Perhaps that was because, when the mouth moved, the sound she heard was deeper and she couldn't smell the milk that signified her mother.

'You called her Eliza?' Mary-Ann asked. She had been standing at the door from the kitchen with tankards of tea in her hands, watching them.

Henry looked at her. 'Yes. She has Eliza's chin and...' His voice cracked and stopped. Placing the cups on the table Mary-Ann went over to him as tears rolled down his cheeks. Thomas was standing at the door unsure what to do.

'Come, take your niece Tom,' Mary-Ann said, 'she's called Eliza.' Henry held the baby out to Thomas and he took her through to the kitchen and sat on the bench next to the sink.

'So you're to be Eliza, little one,' he said softly. As he spoke she recognised that this voice had not spoken to her before.

Three weeks later she was christened. Uncle Robert and his wife Mary brought the family's christening robe and they stood as sponsors, or godparents, to Eliza. As a baby she had no understanding of what was happening to her but she did not cry when the water ran down her head. She was aware that the voices around her sounded odd as they reverberated in the huge space that was St Nicholas' church. Henry beamed at his young family standing on the steps of the font. Thomas, his brother, stood with them but by this time Rachel had already followed her husband to Yorkshire. Mary-Ann smiled at Harry whose eyes rolled into the top of his head as he tried to stand still and yet look up to the roof at the same time. Afterwards they all went back to Robert's cottage next to the yard where they were treated to a generous meal: cold meats and fish with salad from the local nursery, followed by a sumptuous selection of cakes from Boulter's bakers. The adults were sitting outside the door of the cottage which fronted onto the millwright's yard and were positioned at the right point for the spring sunshine to reach them.

'I'm always relieved when that's been done,' said Mary-Ann. 'I don't somehow feel that babes are real people until they've been done in church and the parson's given them back for us to bring up.'

'She's real enough when she's crying,' chuckled Henry.

'Well she was a good girl,' Mary, Robert's wife, commented as she smiled at the sleeping Eliza, 'not like our Edmund. He screamed so you could hardly hear the parson.'

'Always makes sure people know he's there, does our Edmund.' Robert added.

'Yes, he does,' agreed Thomas, 'especially if he doesn't like what's happening.'

Robert looked sideways at Thomas. 'What do you mean?'

'He sulks at the yard when you take Henry with you to assess a job. The younger apprentices laugh at him then – well behind his back at least.'

'Is that so?' replied Robert. 'I do take Henry sometimes. I didn't know Ed sulked though.'

'Yes, he seems to think he ought to go with you each time because…' Thomas faltered as Mary caught his eye.

'Because he's your son,' she finished, 'and so he should.'

'I take the best man for the job, that's how it should be – isn't that right Henry?' Robert's voice was raised. Henry nodded awkwardly. Silence ensued, sharp with tension.

23

Everyone looked at the children who were playing in the yard in an area which had been roped off from the fires and dangerous tools. Harry was trying to roll a metal hoop which Uncle Robert had given him. Four-year-old William thought it was a game. He laughed, chased it and brought it back to Harry each time it fell. Then William caught it while it was still rolling and turned and grinned. He couldn't understand why Harry wasn't very pleased! Tom, who was not quite eighteen months, was trying to keep up with Harry and William and he wobbled.

Mary-Ann laughed, breaking the tension. 'Just look at young Tom – he's a determined one that one – won't accept that he's too young to play.' Tom fell down and started to cry but Carrie went and picked him up. She took him over to the bench where Louisa, with her back to the adults, was embroidering a handkerchief as a surprise for her mother.

'They're good girls, your older two, as well,' said Mary. 'I don't ever remember any of ours caring for each other like that. But then we had a children's nurse to look after the younger ones – I found it too hard as I got older.'

'I'm not surprised these children are good and caring,' suggested Robert, with the voice of someone that feels something strongly and just has to say it. 'I know their father is – look how he stepped in as the man in his own father's household – it takes a certain type of man to do that. I'm proud that you're my nephew. In fact I would go so far as to say I wish you were my son.' At this his wife startled as if he'd hit her but did not speak. Henry and Thomas exchanged glances.

'How is Edmund?' Mary-Ann asked in an attempt to turn the attention away from her husband.

'He's not well,' replied Mary with a controlled evenness of tone. 'He always seems to take a long time to recover.'

'He doesn't fight it when he's ill,' derided Robert. 'He says he's weak and you let him sit there and do everything for him.'

'You know the doctor said his heart doesn't sound right,' she whimpered.

'Doctors,' snorted Robert. 'Take your money and you're still ill.' He grimaced and went out to the privy.

For a few moments there was no conversation and Mary studied her own hands. Then Mary-Ann leant over and placed her hands on top of them. The two Marys looked at each other.

'Is Robert not well either?' Mary-Ann asked, her own eyes filling up in response to the older woman's distress.

Mary shook her head. 'He's always had indigestion. But it's a lot worse now. Doctor said his stomach's not working properly– there's a blockage – too much blood he says. He keeps bleeding him but it's making him weak.'

'Is he taking anything?'

'No. Doctor tried him with acid. Said it would dissolve the blockage. But it hurt so much that he won't take it anymore. The doctor told him that the pain was the blockage coming away but he won't have it.'

'Do you have mint growing?' Mary-Ann asked. Mary shook her head. 'I'll send some up with Henry. Make him some tea with it – oh, and burn his toast,' she added with a little smile.

'He can't eat bread. Says it feels as if it gets stuck.'

'Well, then burn his toast and cut the burnt bits off – it's those bits you want – grind them up fine.' Mary looked surprised so Mary-Ann continued, 'add it to a little water and get him to drink it.'

'Get me to drink what?' Robert asked. He'd just returned and Mary-Ann could sense his pain.

'Water with burnt bread,' replied his wife.

'But –'

'You keep saying the doctors are no good. We'll try this. It's Mary-Ann's suggestion.'

'My mother lives on a farm. They don't have doctors, just ways they've worked out of making things better,' explained Mary-Ann. 'She says that the burnt bits help calm a stomach and take the wind away. It won't taste very nice but I'm also going to send some mint for Mary to make you some tea from.'

Henry looked at his uncle. 'It helps me when I've an upset stomach.'

Thomas laughed. 'He means when he's had too much ale.'

Robert gave a short laugh that didn't reach his eyes. 'Can't be worse than the doctor and his bloodletting I suppose.'

Later the family said goodbye to Robert and Mary and walked home together down Northgate Street. It was late. Henry carried William and Thomas carried young Tom on one shoulder and a flagon of ale in his other hand; Mary-Ann had baby Eliza and Harry walked ahead of them with the girls.

'I wonder what Uncle Robert is thinking,' mused Henry.

'How do you mean?' queried Thomas.

'You know. Wishing I was his son.'

Thomas laughed, 'He just can't help compare you to that scatter-brained idiot.'

Henry frowned. 'No, you're wrong. Ed's no idiot – but he is scatter-brained. I think it's because his head is so full of his own importance that he can't think straight. If he stopped considering himself and looking at others to see how they were looking at him – and then he concentrated at the job he should be doing – he could do it. He's probably quite clever and that's what makes it so difficult.'

'Just keep out of his way,' suggested Mary-Ann.

'There's more to it than that. You see if Uncle Robert's always telling him how good I am,' Henry shrugged, 'and then when he's done something that's not how his father wants it – because Uncle Robert can be hard to please sometimes – he tells him to be more like me. To Ed I must feel like sand in his eye!'

'So that's his problem,' laughed Thomas as he moved Tom onto his other shoulder. 'You know, this young chap's getting heavy. But why are you bothered? Just ignore Ed.'

'I was just thinking. He said he wished I was his son. He's sixty-one and not very well.'

'And? So?' Thomas was struggling to carry Tom and the ale and follow Henry's thoughts and was pleased to find they had arrived home.

'Uncle Robert?' Thomas asked when all the children were upstairs asleep.

'Like I said. He's sixty-one. He doesn't seem well – what could happen tomorrow?'

'Henry my love, are you thinking about his will?' Mary-Ann's voice was strained.

Thomas drew a sharp breath. 'Henry!'

'Yes, his will. Stands to reason. He's talking about wishing I was his son. And he's probably thinking about making a will. Maybe he feels he cannot trust Ed with the yard.'

'Did you notice Aunt Mary when he said it?' Mary-Ann asked and then continued, 'I know she dotes on Edmund. He looks more like her side of the family than the Spandlers. I wouldn't be a bit surprised if she's the reason he's like he is. Be careful Henry.'

'Do you think she'll go home and tell him?' Thomas asked.

'Not exactly. But I think she'll make sure he realises what's at stake.'

'Imagine if he leaves the yard to you,' said Thomas, excited now, 'my brother, the boss! Actually, I think you'd be quite good at it. The younger men come to you for advice.'

'I think you'd both do well to forget the idea,' admonished Mary-Ann, 'or you'll be getting above yourselves. As things stand Uncle Robert is the boss and Edmund looks set to follow him. It's time to stop talking like this.'

'Well I'm stoppin',' said Thomas with a yawn, 'I'm goin' out the back and then to bed.'

'I'm going to read for a bit,' said Henry. Mary-Ann left him on his own and went upstairs to feed Eliza for one last time before she went to bed. Henry picked up his book but it was insufficiently compelling to shut out the events of the day. He tried not to think but it was impossible.

Damn my father! If he'd not gone off to make his fortune he might still have been alive. Robert and Edmund are ill. The yard would have come to me before long and I could have passed it on to the boys. Ed will ruin it! He shivered: the fire had gone out. He picked up the poker. He imagined Edmund's leering, supercilious face and, screwing his eyes tight shut, he jabbed at the fire and riddled the coals furiously as if to erase him. The first thing he saw when he opened his eyes was the flagon. He poured a drink. When he finally retired to bed an hour and a half later, the flagon was empty.

He fell into bed causing Mary-Ann to stir. He wrapped his legs around her and kneaded her breasts with his hands while his mouth sought hers.

She moaned, 'No Henry. It hurts. It's too soon. There's too much milk. And I'm still bleeding Henry. We can't.' His breath caused her to gag. He raised his fist but even through the fog of ale, rage and testosterone he loved his wife. He thumped the bolster next to her. Then he wept. She drew him close and stroked his head. Instantly he fell asleep.

4

Great Yarmouth, the town where they lived, had emerged out of the North Sea many centuries earlier. At first it was merely a strip of sand where fishermen dried their nets and built themselves huts. In medieval times a defensive wall was built around the town in which narrow streets, called Rows, formed, running in an east-west direction down to the river and crossed by two or three wider streets. Many Rows were only three feet wide, some even narrower: consequently sunlight never reached to the ground where the open drain ran. During the first half of the nineteenth century the town prospered and, by the time of baby Eliza's birth, outgrew the walls. New, grand, ornate public buildings were being built and parks laid out.

A mill at the intersection of Nelson Road and Crown Road was in the way and the owners were offered a good hand of money for the land. They came to Robert asking him to demolish the mill and build it elsewhere: he suggested that the working part of the mill could be moved without dismantling it and over the previous weeks they had been busy with preparations. A base had been built at the new site on the Denes north of the town and the cap and sails had been removed and were being stored at the yard. Three troll cart owners had been well paid in readiness for the day. Troll carts were a special cart used in the Rows, built with the wheels under the load-bearing area which was nearly a yard wide and almost two yards long: three carts side by side would make one large area without any gaps.

'Are you coming to see?' Henry asked on the morning of the move.

'Will it be safe?' Mary-Ann asked in reply.

'Yes, just keep well back near the buildings. We're using three carts so it will be quite wide.'

'Probably be better near a side turning then. How many men?'

'All of us I think. Uncle Robert has planned it. Says it should work.'

'Has it ever been done before?' Henry shook his head. This would be a difficult job.

'Buy your biscuits here!' Boulters the bakers, whose premises were at the end of Row Three not far from Spandlers yard, were quick to take the opportunity to sell and they weren't the only ones making money: word had spread and the many sightseers brought out what seemed to be an equal amount of street traders. There was a carnival feeling about the day: a man on stilts was telling jokes on one street corner; a juggler was entertaining on another; one enterprising family was selling hot potatoes; shrimp sellers vied for the best pitch and, amongst the crowd, an older lady and a young girl skilfully removed valuables from pockets.

Mary-Ann, with two-month-old Eliza tied on her chest and holding the hands of William and Tom, was looking towards the mill. A tripod was being lifted and moved into position by six of Spandler's men.

'That'll never hold the mill,' a man nearby said in a loud voice and the crowd laughed. Robert glared and the laughter died away. Mary-Ann looked more closely at it: it was taller than the mill and had a pulley hanging from a rotating arm at its apex. Struts could be seen strengthening the triangle which formed the base but it did not seem wide enough: surely the weight of the mill would cause it to topple? She was anxious. Then, once it was in position, the men started rolling some long, stout tree trunks towards it.

'Now what are they doing?' shouted another voice from the crowd with a look towards the first heckler.

'Dunno,' shouted someone else, 'you never can tell with these Spandlers. Be something clever for sure.' The crowd went quiet as they watched. The men attached a trunk to one side of the base. One end of the trunk was level with the corner of the base and the other end stuck out beyond the base for a distance that was at least as long as the tripod was tall. Mary-Ann smiled to herself as she realised what they were doing. Two more trunks were attached to the other two sides, each one sticking out beyond the base like the first one, effectively making the base very wide. Then, to increase the weight at the base, another trunk was positioned on top of each of the bottom ones. They were attached with cast iron bolts that Thomas had designed and made specifically for this task so that the whole thing took less than an hour. The crowd applauded.

Next one of the younger apprentices climbed up the inside the mill and out onto the platform. There was no sound as the crowd watched him many feet above them. He attached the hook on the arm at the apex of the tripod to struts that had been fixed inside the top of the mill and a few minutes later, having climbed back down, he appeared at street level: the crowd applauded once more and for a moment he looked surprised but then grinned and took a bow. Further struts had been fixed lower down inside the mill to strengthen the structure and Robert went inside for one last check. As he reappeared he nodded to Henry.

'Pull,' shouted Henry to the men by the pulley. They pulled together, kept in time by Henry. The crowd went quiet again and the wood creaked. The mill began to rise off its base, crookedly.

'Stop!' Robert shouted, 'she's still attached. Lower her gently.' Men rushed to where Robert was pointing with hammers and picks to chip away the remaining mortar.

'No wonder she was creaking. That could have ripped her apart,' commented Henry.

Robert nodded. 'It was a close thing. But it didn't. Now let's try again.'

'Pull,' called Henry, 'Pull.' Slowly the mill inched into the air whilst the trundle carts backed in close to the tripod.

'Hold,' called Henry after the mill had risen about a foot from the base. They had reached a very dangerous part but in spite of this the crowd were edging forward as they jostled for position. 'Ready to move?'

'Yes,' shouted the men holding the rope. Mary-Ann, realising that if something went wrong the mill would probably fall on Henry, felt sick and wished she had not come.

'One.' The men on the pulley took a small step to the left.

'Two,' and they moved their right legs. Slowly, as the count continued, the arm at the top of the tripod swivelled round pulling the huge mill with it. People gawped, open-mouthed. By the time Henry reached ten the mill was positioned over the carts.

'It'll break them,' a voice called from the crowd and Robert glared again. The three cart-owners looked sideways at each other as they tried to keep their horses calm and steady: they were being paid well for this job, but it wouldn't cover the cost of replacing their carts if they broke. A few minutes later the mill had settled and the carts held. The young apprentice climbed the tripod and unhitched the pulley: this time he looked crestfallen when there was no applause but the crowd were too taken up with the sight of a mill balanced on three carts to watch him.

'Move,' ordered Robert. The three carters urged their horses forward but the one on the left stood still causing a jolt: the mill tottered. Onlookers nearby scattered and an old woman fell. Instead of trying to get to her feet she curled herself into a ball and covered her head with her arms.

'You told me there would be no problem getting them to move together,' Robert hissed at the carter's leader, anxiety making his voice acerbic.

Several men from the crowd went to the old woman and lifted her out of the way, still curled in a ball. She wailed as the men put her down in a doorway and, because her eyes were still tightly shut, did not know it was the doorway of an inn. The landlord appeared to be about to move her on when a well-dressed young man from the crowd came and spoke with him. Moments later a serving girl came out with a tankard of ale. She crouched down next to the old woman who opened her eyes, grinned and very quickly recovered.

Robert looked at Henry, 'That could have been bad.'

'They're too near,' replied Henry. He raised his voice towards the crowd, 'You saw what happened. You need to move back.' The crowd jeered but still shuffled back a few feet.

The carter's leader turned to Robert, 'If some of the men could push from the back, just to get them started, that would help.' The horses were scrawny, poorly fed animals and struggled with the weight. The men pushed and the animals moved forward but as soon as the men stopped so did the animals. In the end the only way to continue to move was with the men pushing the backs of the carts all the time. Progress was slow and exhausting. The crowd very quickly lost interest and disappeared. By the time the sun was setting they had only moved three hundred yards. The men were hot, dusty, sweaty and discouraged. Robert had expected them to reach the new site that day but they were less than a third of the way there. Henry was grim. Thomas, having been part of the group that had gone ahead with the tripod to prepare the new site, came to see what was happening. Although he knew the mill would be on the carts, the sight was so odd that he stopped and stared for a moment. Then he started walking round the mill.

'This is going to take a lot longer than you thought,' said Henry to Robert, 'and we'll have to pay some of the men to guard the mill and carts tonight.' The carters had unhitched their horses and gone, but not before negotiating an increased fee for the following day.

'I know,' replied Robert, his voice cracked with weariness and strain. 'I should have hired the carts from the brewery. At least their horses are well-fed and used to heavy loads.'

'Where's Edmund been today?'

'In the office updating the ledgers. When his mother heard what we were doing she forbade his taking part. Too dangerous. Actually,' Robert sighed, 'it was his idea to use the troll carts. Said we'd save some money.'

'But it's going to cost us more than we saved! Why didn't you include me in the discussion?'

'His mother says I favour you. Treat you like a partner rather than an employee. Said I should listen to my son more.'

'Well make sure she knows how much his latest–'

'Come and look at this,' Thomas shouted. He had crouched down to look underneath the carts. As Henry and Robert crouched next to him he continued, 'the weight's too much for them. See. It's bending the axles. As soon as we start to move tomorrow they will break.'

'Well we can't bring the men and the tripod back now, it's going dark. It would be too dangerous,' said Robert.

'What are we going to do?' Thomas asked. Robert and Henry shrugged. The three of them remained crouching by the mill, their minds numb, unable to think. Silence engulfed them like a blanket.

'We're back boss.' The unexpected voice made them jump and Robert fell against Henry. They laughed, breaking the silence: the blanket vanished.

'Now you're here we'll leave,' Robert said to the three brothers who had been assigned the night watch. 'You'll be paid more than your normal rate for this, you realise that don't you?'

The men grinned and looked at each other. 'We didn't,' said the oldest of the three, 'thank you.'

Robert turned to his two nephews. 'Come down to me after you've been home and had a bite. Think while you eat and bring any ideas. We'll work it out over some ale next door.' Robert's cottage and the yard were next to the King's Arms.

Thomas and Henry walked home as quickly as they could. As soon as they entered the house they could smell fried fish.

'Gosh. I'm really hungry!' Thomas exclaimed.

'And me,' replied Henry, raising his voice towards the kitchen, 'That smells good.'

Mary-Ann poked her head round the kitchen door. 'I had an idea that you'd be home more hungry than usual,' she said. 'Come on, move your books, it's time to eat,' she added to the older children.

The room where they were about to eat was simply furnished but quite comfortable: along one wall a fire burned and arranged round the fire were three wooden chairs for which Mary-Ann had made cushions. The one on the right was a rocking chair that had belonged to Henry's mother. Immediately behind the one in the middle was a long table where Louisa, Carrie and Harry had been doing their school work but they lost no time in clearing it away. Louisa reached up to a rack above their heads and lifted down the plates while Carrie took from a cupboard beneath a large earthenware mug in which were all the knives and forks and placed it on the table. There was one bench already at the table and the other one just needed sliding along from by the fire which Harry did, turning the middle chair round to face the table at the same time. Harry and

William sat along one side with two-year-old Tom between them and Louisa and Carrie sat along the other side with Thomas. Henry pulled one of the remaining two chairs to the other end of the table and sat down.

'Girls, can you help me bring things through?' Mary-Ann called from the kitchen. A few moments later Louisa and Carrie reappeared carrying a huge tin of baked potatoes and a bowl of mixed carrots and swede: steam rose from both. They were closely followed by Mary-Ann with a large pan of fish: these were not whole fish but bits of broken fish that would not sell in the shops and which she'd purchased cheaply from the quayside. She put the fish on the plates, giving Henry and Thomas a carefully browned cod's head each as well, as these were considered special.

'What time did you leave?' Thomas asked Mary-Ann after they been eating a few minutes and had assuaged the worst of their hunger.

'Oh about ten minutes after you finally started moving. When everyone realised how slowly you were going most people went home. How far did you get?'

'Only as far as where St Nicholas' road crosses over,' replied Henry in a monotone.

'– and that's not the only problem,' added Thomas, 'since we stopped moving the axles of the carts are bending. If we try and move tomorrow they will snap like twigs.'

'What are you going to do?'

'We're meeting in the King's Arms with Uncle Robert now to see if we can work out a way forward.' There was silence for a few minutes while everyone ate.

'Pa?' Harry queried and Henry nodded permission to speak. He was very strict about there not being lots of childish babble at mealtimes. 'Mr Mounseer was telling us about the Egyptians today.'

'And?' Henry's questioning tone suggested that there had better be more to it than that if Harry was disturbing the meal.

'W-Well when they were building the p-p-pyramids they used rollers to move the heavy slabs of s-stone,' stuttered Harry.

Henry looked puzzled but Thomas grinned and looked from him to Harry. 'He doesn't follow you.' He paused. 'The mill?'

Then it was Henry's turn to grin and he put his knife and fork down with an uncharacteristic clatter. 'Could we do it? How did they do it?'

'They put four or five rollers under each slab and pulled it,' explained Harry, stutter-less and confident now under the beams of delight radiating from the two men. 'The rollers turned and the slab moved forward on top of them. When a roller reached the back of the slab it was lifted and moved to the front.'

'I see,' said Henry, 'Come on, eat up Thomas. Can't wait to tell Uncle Robert. Well done Harry for speaking up.' Harry grinned.

Half an hour later Henry and Thomas walked into the King's Arms. Sitting in one of the alcoves were Uncle Robert and Edmund.

'I see Mummy's boy is joining us,' muttered Thomas. They walked to the bar.

'Thanks for coming,' said Robert as they sat down, 'but Edmund has an idea that he says will work.' Henry and Thomas looked at each other.

Edmund wriggled in his seat in an effort to look down on his cousins: it irked him that they were taller than he was. Henry couldn't help thinking how childish Edmund looked next to Thomas in spite of being older by four years. His round, perspiring face was shiny in the gaslight.

'I think,' he squeaked, and then stopped. He cleared his throat. 'I think we should lift the mill and then rotate the axles on the carts so that the bend is pointing upwards. Then gently lower it until the axles straighten. Then we'll need to raise it again for the drivers to move the carts forward about ten yards to free them up. Then all we need do is back them in again and set off as before.'

'If we set off and the axles then break, which I think they will, we'll end up paying for repairs,' countered Henry.

'That's if the carters back the carts in again. Once they're out from under the mill they'll be off,' added Thomas, 'besides which it takes too long. It'll take us another two days to reach the new site.'

'But you said it was a good idea,' whined Edmund to his father.

'I said I couldn't think of anything else,' replied Robert with a sigh. 'Have you two a better idea?' Then he relaxed and smiled: the two brothers were grinning.

'It was our Harry actually –'

'A child,' snorted Edmund.

'Be quiet,' ordered his father. 'Let us hear it.'

By the time Henry had finished the explanation, Robert was also grinning.

Edmund looked peeved and objected, 'But you've already committed to using the carts tomorrow. We'll have to pay them.'

'Yes,' replied Robert patiently, 'we can attach their horses directly to the mill. They can pull it, as we don't have hordes of slaves like the Egyptians.'

Edmund scowled. 'Well I don't think that'll work.' He smiled as if he'd suddenly remembered something. 'Besides which we've only another three tree trunks at the yard and even they still have stumps of branches attached to them. We can't use the ones on the tripod because we will need it to lift the mill onto the rollers.'

'We'll come at first light tomorrow and make the trunks smooth.'

'We don't have enough trunks I tell you!' Edmund had turned his face close to Henry's and raised his voice. Henry blinked and looked at Robert.

'Three's enough,' replied Robert, his voice deliberately low and even. 'We can lower the mill onto those and then we can take one or two more off the tripod. Thanks to Thomas here they'll come off and go back on easily. The joints were well designed and casted and work well.' Thomas grinned and nodded his head.

'Why do you never say anything I do is good,' objected Edmund, standing up. 'Ma's right. You think more of them than me. But I'm your son. I'm going home.'

'No,' said Robert, still not raising his voice. 'Sit down.' Edmund glared at his father and it appeared for a moment as if he was going to go but then he slumped back down, making the bench rock.

Robert continued: 'I'm losing my patience with you. Your insistence on using the troll carts has cost us time and money. Can't you just see that this new plan is good? That's why we'll use it, not because I prefer these two. Are you coming in early tomorrow to help prepare the rollers?' Edmund just stared at his father. 'I thought not. They also work harder than you do. You may go.' Edmund looked at his cousins: his lips parted malevolently and he left.

The rollers worked so well that by the following night they had reached the new site. The morning after everyone from the yard was there, together with a crowd of onlookers including Mary-Ann, watching as they moved the mill onto the base. A cheer went up as the owners entered the mill.

'That was hard work. I hope we never have to do anything like that again,' commented Henry as he and Thomas made their way back to the yard.

'Where's Edmund this morning? I didn't expect him earlier when we were working but I thought he might turn up at the end.'

'Oh, I asked Uncle Robert. Apparently he has a migraine and his mother says he needs to stay indoors. I say he's sulking at home.'

Thomas nodded. 'Thanks to him I can't think that the yard made much money out of all that work – what with paying to have the carts repaired.'

'Do you think that's what happened? They were being paid well and the axles didn't actually break.'

'The carters were very angry. Apparently they didn't straighten properly so the carts went up and down as they rolled along. Whatever they put on top rolled off into the gutter.'

Henry laughed. 'Uncle Robert will have offered to repair the carts at the yard and not given them the extra they asked for on the second day. He's more than a match for any angry carter!'

Just at that moment a young lady crossed the road towards them as if she was going to talk to them but then, with a glance at Thomas, carried on without stopping.

Henry looked sideways at Thomas. 'And who was that then?' Thomas coloured but said nothing. 'She certainly looked at you.'

Silence. Then Thomas blurted. 'We're walking out together,'

'Seriously?'

Thomas nodded. 'I'm very fond of her.'

'So,' Henry paused and smiled, 'my little brother has a lady. When do we get to meet her?'

'Tonight.' He gave a short laugh. 'I'll bring her round tonight.'

5

Thomas had finished preparing the moulds ready for the next casting. He glanced from the gate of the yard to the cottage. The first room on the right was the office where his uncle would be sitting at the large desk checking the hours the men had worked that week in readiness for the following day when he would give each man his wages.

He drew a deep breath as he entered the office. His uncle glanced at him as he walked in but then returned to a column of figures in the ledger. Thomas let out his breath silently and waited. Eventually Robert put down his quill and looked at him.

'Do you have another task for me today? The moulds are ready to take the iron tomorrow.'

His uncle smiled. 'Is this a request to leave early? Henry's still supervising the wood at the station, you know?'

'Yes, he knows I won't be waiting for him tonight. I've someone else to see first, before I go home,' explained Thomas.

Robert picked up his pen again. 'You've damped the furnace down and released the steam in the boiler?' Thomas nodded. 'Then go.'

Thomas walked down through St Nicholas' churchyard and out of the gate in the east wall. He turned right and immediately before him was a large building: he considered it ugly because it had an iron roof and bare brick. He waited for ten minutes, solitary and still: then double doors clanked and, suddenly, as if a sluice gate had been opened, the street was flooded with people. For twenty yards he was carried along involuntarily until the crowd thinned enough for him to stand still, although people still surged around him. He panicked for a moment. He turned around and just at that moment Matilda reached him. They both gasped and he fell into place alongside her.

'Uncle Robert let me leave early. Henry worked out there was a connection when you walked past us this morning. He wants to meet you and I've said I'll take you round tonight.'

'Tonight!'

'Yes. That's if Rosina will look after your mother.'

'Don't suppose that'll be a problem. It's just so sudden.'

'You've known that it would have to happen eventually.'

'I just hope they like me. What if they don't?'

'I'm sure they will. But he's my brother, not my father, remember?'

'I know but I should hate it if you fell out over me.' She smiled at Thomas who briefly took hold of her hand and squeezed it. He let go but they walked along closely, very closely, cutting through to Market Gates and across Market Place to Row fifty-four. Her home was a typical Row house with a privy in the back courtyard shared with other houses. There was a room on the ground floor from which a steep spiral staircase led up to another room. In the centre of that room another small staircase led up to the attic and this was where she lived.

Later at Francis Buildings the younger children were in bed and Mary-Ann was cleaning the hearth. 'This is strange,' she said to Henry, 'your brother bringing his girl home to us – like as if we were his parents.' Henry looked up from his boots. Part of the seam had worked loose and he was mending it.

'Well I suppose I'm as near to a father as he'll ever remember.' He looked over to his eldest son. 'Harry's still up?' he queried.

Mary-Ann nodded. 'I told him he could stay and say hello but then had to quickly take himself off to bed.'

'Louisa? Carrie?'

'They've gone to visit Aunt Hannah. There were fresh spices at the market today and the girls have made her some gingers.'

Henry smiled. 'She likes them. I think it's because she's so old – they're something she can taste. She'll enjoy their company. I'm sure she misses Rachel.' Just then the front door opened and Thomas and Matilda entered. There was a moment of awkward silence during which Henry and Mary-Ann both glanced at the young woman: she met their eyes.

'Henry, Mary, I'd like you to meet Matilda.'

Henry held out a hand. 'He's told you I'm his brother?' he asked. Matilda took his hand, nodded imperceptibly and quickly looked at Thomas. Mary-Ann smiled but said nothing. Harry stood up from Thomas's chair where he'd been sitting.

'It's alright Harry, you stay there,' said Thomas as he sat down on the children's bench and pulled Matilda down next to him. Harry hesitated, unsure whether Thomas had just allowed him to stay up a while longer.

'Now Harry, say your greeting,' directed Mary-Ann.

'Nice to meet you,' said Harry, holding out his hand in imitation of his father. Matilda, from her seat on the bench, looked up into the deep brown eyes of the serious looking seven-year-old. She took his hand.

'It's a pleasure to meet you, young sir,' she said, smiling. Harry grinned, causing his nose to wrinkle and showing the gaps where his milk teeth had come out.

'You'll be my new aunt soon, won't you?'

Matilda blushed and looked at Thomas.

'Come on son, time for bed. You're embarrassing our guest,' said Henry. Harry fumbled with the door that led to the stairs then scampered up them. The adults laughed, the earlier awkwardness gone.

'What do you do?' Henry asked.

'I'm a warper in the silk factory.'

This impressed Mary-Ann who used to work there; she knew how the quality of a finished piece of silk was affected by the skill of the warper. 'You're happy there?' she asked.

'It pays well and I enjoy working with the other girls.'

'With some satisfaction, I'm sure,' suggested Henry.

'Well, yes. It's good when the weavers all want to use the loom that you've set up. Makes you feel as if you're doing a good job,' she hesitated, 'but it's not what I really want to do. I've helped at a few births. I'd like to study so I would really know what I was doing. Then I could help women and their babies.'

'Won't pay as well,' Mary-Ann pointed out.

'No, I know. It wouldn't be for years yet.'

'You live in Yarmouth?'

'Yes,' replied Matilda, 'I live with my elderly mother…'

'Her mother's seventy-one and frail and has lost the use of her legs. She doesn't really know herself anymore,' Thomas explained.

'That's sad. Does she know who you are?' Mary-Ann asked.

'Sometimes,' Matilda shrugged, 'but not always.'

'Matilda cares for her,' continued Thomas. 'It's hard – Matilda struggles to lift her in spite of her being frail and old.'

'What happens during the day when you're at work?'

'My sister Rosina and her family live downstairs. They have six children, all young. She keeps an eye on her during the day. But it will help having Thomas there. We have to take water all the way up to the attic to clean her and Rosina's husband is often away. He's a seaman,' she added in answer to Henry questioning look.

'You said "having Thomas there"?' Mary-Ann asked.

'Yes,' Thomas hesitated but then drew a deep breath, 'I'm going to move in with them.' Thomas, looked from Mary-Ann to Henry and back again.

'More room for us,' laughed Mary-Ann, 'but we'll miss you.'

Ten months passed. It was now late spring 1852 and the wedding was set for the thirteenth of May. One evening Henry was reading aloud from a book; Mary-Ann, Louisa and Carrie had been mending but as the light faded they'd just put it aside when suddenly the door opened and Thomas and Matilda walked in. Everyone stood up and there was much laughter as they hugged each other.

'William, Rosina's husband, is home from sea. They're looking after mother tonight,' explained Matilda. 'We wanted to ask you something.'

'We'd like you to come and see us wed.' said Thomas. 'You know, come to the church,' he explained as Henry looked puzzled.

'But what about the wedding breakfast?' Mary-Ann asked. 'I always thought that I would do that.'

'Yes,' said Matilda, 'perhaps we could have the breakfast as a picnic? After the service Thomas and I'll go down to the beach. The younger children could come with us and you and the older ones could fetch the picnic and follow us down.' She paused, looking from Mary-Ann to Henry and then back to Mary-Ann again. 'Oh, please say yes. We want you to share our day.'

Mary-Ann smiled and nodded. 'It would certainly be different.'

'We did a lot of our courting on the beach,' said Thomas by way of an explanation.

Henry looked at Mary-Ann, his eyes crinkling at the corners. 'So did we actually.' All four of them laughed.

'What about your mother?'

'She wouldn't know what was going on and it would probably upset her to be moved from the attic,' replied Matilda.

'Besides which, she's not well. Not eating much and sleeping a lot,' added Thomas.

Mary-Ann nodded. 'Best not to disturb her then.'

The wedding day arrived, a day that, in the years to come, Mary-Ann looked back upon wistfully. The children were good during the service, awed by the church just as they'd been for Eliza's christening. Everyone enjoyed the picnic on the beach and Mary-Ann thought that Henry was at last losing the sadness that had been so much a part of him when she first met him: he was clearly enjoying his younger brother's happiness. A couple of days later Thomas asked if he could move back in: Matilda's sister and her husband wanted to put some of their children in the attic and had decided to bring the old lady downstairs. Thomas was expecting to finish his apprenticeship by the end of the year and they would find their own place then.

That summer was a happy time in Francis Buildings, although the small house was very crowded: Thomas and Matilda had a small sleeping area in the attic; Mary-Ann and Henry had one bedroom with Eliza and Tom sleeping with them and the older girls and boys were in the other bedroom with a curtain dividing them.

Time continued; the year aged; the heat from the sun weakened – and happiness began to show its frailty. One evening in late October Thomas and Matilda didn't immediately sit down after the meal had been cleared away and the younger children had been put to bed.

'We're going out,' said Thomas, 'down to the beach.'

Mary-Ann frowned. 'It's going dark?'

'I know,' replied Thomas.

'Apparently there's going to be a bonfire down there,' explained Matilda, 'with free chestnuts.' At this Harry looked up from the book he was reading but a quick glance at his mother told him that there was no point in asking.

'Sounds good,' said Henry, 'but who's supplying the chestnuts?'

'Some new group. From America I think,' replied Thomas. 'There's going to be entertainment and I'm sure there'll be opportunity to watch the hecklers. I don't mind what they do so long as the chestnuts are good.' They all laughed.

No-one realised how that evening would change their lives.

'Well I have mending to do to keep me company, so I don't mind if you all go,' suggested Mary-Ann. Harry again looked hopeful.

Thomas noticed. 'There's no school tomorrow. Can he come mother?'

Mary-Ann looked at her son. 'Yes, go on then.' Harry jumped up with excitement. 'But mind you stay close to the others. You don't want to get lost in the dark.'

They returned two hours later, having eaten their fill of chestnuts, with Harry asleep on his father's shoulders. Henry took him straight up to bed while Mary-Ann made tea.

'It was really good. There were jugglers and we played games.' Matilda told her

'We also sang,' added Carrie, 'Mostly religious, but easy with nice tunes. Some rounds which were fun – one of them the parts came in very quickly after each other and made you feel as if you were falling over the people in front even though you were singing and not walking.'

'Lots of chestnuts,' said Thomas, patting his stomach.

'Yes and a blackberry drink with it. Only one beaker but it was nice – then there was hot water,' said Louisa, 'but no tea.'

'Or ale,' added Henry and everyone laughed. 'Apparently they don't drink either, so it wouldn't do for me.'

'I thought it was interesting, what they were saying,' said Matilda, 'although I'm a bit confused. Something about a new prophet in America whom they say God has sent because the churches have gone wrong.'

Mary-Ann looked surprised. 'I'm sure the vicar would have something to say about that.'

'Mmm, probably. But I can see what they were getting at – just how bothered are the churchwardens and the vicar and those like them?' Matilda asked. 'Those who are really poor have to stand at the back, especially at Harvest or Christmas, while some of the pews are empty.'

'It's not that long ago that the number of free seats was increased,' said Henry. 'We don't have a lot of money but we pay our pew rent. There are a lot of those sitting on the free seats who could pay.'

'Why should anyone pay to sit down in church?' Matilda was a tall lady and everyone was awed by her unusually raised voice and red face. 'Did you know an old man from our Row collapsed and died during the service at Easter? No, I think they're only interested in those who have money – so that the church can have some of it.'

Henry held up his hands. 'You're quite fierce, Matilda, when you get excited about something. What did you think, Thomas?'

'Well,' he replied, 'they also said that there could be opportunities in America for some people.' Henry raised his eyebrows at Thomas's statement.

'Who?' he asked.

Thomas shrugged, not meeting his brother's gaze. 'Those who are interested I suppose.'

6

A few weeks later Mary-Ann started feeling sick. At first she put it down to the handful of shrimps that young Phoebe from next door had given her when they'd walked home together from outside the fish market at the corner of the market square. It was Phoebe's usual pitch from where she sold the shrimps and those she'd given Mary-Ann were her last at the end of the day. Mary-Ann had smelt them carefully before she'd eaten them and had felt fine, but now she was queasy. She made herself some mint tea, thinking that it would settle down. However a few days later she was vomiting first thing in the morning and her breasts itched: wearily, she realised she was pregnant.

As soon as she told Matilda Thomas suggested that Matilda stopped working and helped Mary-Ann. He had just finished his apprenticeship and so was now being paid more. Matilda very quickly took on the running of the house: Mary-Ann was clearly finding it difficult.

'What's up?' Henry asked one evening as he looked at his wife rubbing her back, her forehead knotted into a frown.

'I don't know. This is not like any of my other babies.'

'You mean there's something wrong?' Alarm registered in Henry's eyes as he remembered William's birth.

'I'm not bleeding or anything like that. It's just that it's so hard. Perhaps because I'm older. Thank goodness Matilda's here.' She smiled at her sister-in-law.

Although Eliza would still sometimes snuggle up next to her mother she very quickly learnt that if she needed something to go to Matilda whom she called Da. One evening she looked at Matilda and said, 'Da,' and then at her father and said, 'Pa,' then at Matilda, 'Da, Da,' and her father again, 'Pa, Pa,' 'Da, Da,' 'Pa, Pa,'... everyone was laughing.

'Stop 'liza. I can't laugh any more,' said Matilda, wiping the tears from her eyes. Eliza reached up to her and Matilda bent down and picked her up. Eliza buried her face in Matilda's hair and hugged her. Then she looked up and around the room at her family who were all talking to each other and not looking at her any more. It didn't matter. Although only fifteen months old she knew she was very happy.

As the pregnancy continued Mary-Ann grew big, very big. At the end of the second week in January, Abigail, Mary-Ann's mother, came to visit. Shortly after her arrival she took her daughter upstairs and when they returned half an hour later Mary-Ann had been crying.

'I can't be absolutely sure,' said Abigail, 'but I think there's more than one baby in there.' Fleetingly Henry looked delighted but his face froze as he looked at his mother-in-law. She continued, 'My older sister was Mary-Ann's age when she carried two. She and the babies died.' The adults went quiet and the only sounds were the children playing.

Henry went to his wife and wrapped his arms around her as if he could somehow protect her from what was to come. 'What would I do if...'

'I'm not planning on going,' said Mary-Ann, smiling at him with watery eyes.

'What about the children?' Henry's voice betrayed his tension.

'There's Matilda,' said Thomas.

'She'll want her own family soon enough,' said Henry with a look at the younger couple.

'But we wouldn't leave you without help,' said Matilda with Thomas nodding a little hesitantly.

'Thank you – but listen – you're all talking as if I am going to die,' said Mary-Ann, shaking her head, 'and I said I'm not.'

No-one spoke as Mary-Ann held Henry's gaze. They stood, frozen by a chill that this time enveloped the children who stopped their play and stared at the adults. Eliza moved first, toddling over to them. Matilda picked her up.

'You must be careful,' said Abigail to Mary-Ann, 'certainly no lifting. Not even Eliza.'

Mary-Ann nodded as Matilda spoke. 'She comes to me a lot of the time.'

'And Matilda does most of the cooking now. Louisa helps with the shopping,' added Mary-Ann.

'That's good. How far are you now?'

'Five months.'

'In another month start to lie down every afternoon. Even if you don't sleep. Eat as well as you can.'

'I get full very easily – and then I get sick if I try to eat any more.'

Abigail turned to Matilda. 'Give her four or five small meals a day, not big at all.' Matilda nodded, putting her free arm round her sister-in-law. Eliza looked from Matilda to her mother and stroked her mother's hair.

Mary-Ann reached up and ran her finger down Eliza's nose. 'You know there's something wrong, don't you little one?' Mary-Ann looked at Matilda. 'I'm so fortunate to have you,' she said wiping away tears yet again.

'You're very special to me,' Matilda replied. 'You've always made me feel part of your family. You know I can never remember feeling a stranger here, not even that first evening.'

In February winds screeched in from the North Sea, bringing with them heavy rain. Combining with the pull of the moon they dragged the sea up onto the dunes where it formed large breakers and splashed and frothed as if it was establishing its territory. The people of Great Yarmouth watched warily, hearing stories of floods beyond Caister from the few soggy individuals who made the difficult journey across the marshes. A few days of such weather were welcomed because the muck in the open drains of the Rows was washed away by the wind and rain, making whole town smell sweeter. However, the people knew the destructive power of the sea and many of the worshippers at Nicholas' church that weekend sought God that He might keep the sea within its boundary.

'Shut that door quickly,' said Matilda as Harry and William came in from school, 'I think it's going colder out there.'

'Anything to eat?' Harry asked hopefully as they went upstairs to change out of their stiff school collars and shirts, hanging them up carefully so that they would pass inspection tomorrow. By the time they came down Matilda had spread the last two slices from yesterday's bread with bacon fat. It was quite stale but the boys hardly noticed. After they had finished, which wasn't long, they took the slops out and fetched more water.

'Here you are, drink these,' said Matilda when they'd finished, handing them two steaming cups of tea. Both boys grimaced as the hot cups touched their cold hands.

The front door opened.

'Cayyie!' Eliza called from the pen in the corner.

Carrie, removing her hat and shaking the rain out of her fringe, ignored her, 'Where's Ma?

'Resting,' replied Matilda.

Caroline grinned at Matilda, 'I've just passed my school test so I can move to the seniors next week. I wanted to tell her.' She walked over to Eliza and Tom, crouched down and gave them both a hug. For a moment Eliza's face lit up until she realised that Carrie wasn't going to pick her up.

'Aren't you clever – you must have worked hard for that – but why not leave it until your father gets in and tell them both together when your mother comes down to eat?' Matilda suggested and then turned to the two boys. 'Could you look in on old Mrs Johnson and see if she needs more coal on her fire? And ask her if she wants a fishcake because there's plenty. Tell her it's from your mother because she'll not know who I am.' The boys nodded and went out. They turned right and walked quickly past their window and in through the next front door. This one did not lead into a living area like theirs but instead there was a narrow passage which led past a room lined with shelves containing baskets of all shapes and sizes.

'Hello Mr Shuckford,' the boys called out. The basket-maker, father of Phoebe the shrimp-seller, grinned at the boys as they walked past.

'Hello boys,' Mrs Shuckford appeared at the top of the stairs, peering down at them. 'I saw to her fire about half an hour ago but I'm sure she'd like to see you.'

'Ma has a fish cake for her,' called back William. The boys listened outside a door at the end of the passage and could hear a loud clicking sound. Knowing there was no point in knocking because they wouldn't be heard, they pushed the door open. Their eyes were immediately drawn to a length of cord hung over a hook in the ceiling, one end of which had been wound onto a reel. In front of the free end sat a woman: she was leaning down towards the floor moving the large wooden bobbins that were attached to it so quickly that it was impossible to count the number. The boys moved forward and, suddenly aware of them, she stopped.

'Hands not too bad today Mrs Johnson?' Harry asked.

'Smorning,' she nodded, 'but hurtin' now.' She rubbed her hands together.

William looked at her knobbly joints. 'Shall I ask mother if she has any of that cream that Grandma makes?'

'And mother says to ask if you'd like a fish cake. She's made plenty,' added Harry.

She nodded. 'She's allus kind, yar maw. Here, tek me dish,' she said as she wound the completed cord onto the reel so that the bobbins rose from near the floor to above her head. William picked the dish up from her table.

'I'll fill your kettle and then Carrie'll make you some tea when she comes,' said Harry. As the boys left she stretched up towards the bobbins and as they walked down the passage they could hear the clicking again.

They reached home at the same time as Louisa.

'Where have you been?' Harry asked.

'We've been home from school ages,' added William.

'I'll tell you later.' Louisa grinned. 'Along with everyone else.'

An hour later Henry and Thomas arrived back from work. The living space erupted into laughter and talking: Henry lifted Eliza out of the pen and swung her around; Thomas played with the boys on the floor and Carrie and Louisa were talking with Matilda who started to fry the fish cakes. Soon the smell reached Henry's nostrils.

'I'll go and wake Mary-Ann,' Henry said.

'I don't suppose she's still asleep,' laughed Matilda looking around the room. As he went upstairs Carrie slipped out with the fishcake for Mrs Johnson. By the time she returned everyone was seated at the table.

'Come on, I'm hungry,' said young Tom with a cheeky grin at his older sister. There was silence for a few minutes while everyone ate.

'Pa, I have some news,' said Louisa.

'Yes,' said Henry, nodding.

'I'm fourteen next week and Mrs Fielding at school says that I am ready for work. She told me that Boulters were taking on an assistant in the shop. I called in on my way home and I can start next week'

This news shocked Carrie who was now upset because Louisa wouldn't be at the senior department when she started. Eliza, who was sitting between her two big sisters, realised there was something wrong by the stiffening of Carrie's body and leant her head against her but Carrie nudged her away. Mary-Ann noticed this and frowned.

'So, is that what you want to do, work in the baker's shop?' Henry asked.

Louisa shrugged. 'Mrs Fielding says I may get a chance to help with the baking. And she says I'm good at that.'

Matilda noticed Carrie's face and suddenly remembered her news. 'I think Carrie has something to tell us.'

'I-I-I I've passed my school test. I-I can go to the seniors next week.' Carrie started to cry. She'd been so excited about it when she came in and now she wished it wasn't happening.

'That's wonderful,' said Mary-Ann but Louisa felt that Carrie was spoiling her moment.

'Oh, she's scared,' she derided, but at glance from her father she stopped.

'I think we will finish our meal,' said Henry. Silence returned, only broken by the occasional sniff from Carrie.

Later, after the younger children had gone to bed, Henry and Thomas went out for a walk. It had been Thomas's suggestion and Henry felt he wanted to talk about something. Matilda was in the back kitchen cleaning the ash and dust from the floor and the small range so she had shut the door. Mary-Ann was in the living area stitching Henry's new shirt for later in the year and thinking, not for the first time, how much easier it would be with one of those new machines for sewing. She looked up at her daughters who were also sewing. They were working on things from the mending basket which contained clothes that needed repair and altering. Louisa was putting new cuffs on one of William's old shirts ready for when Tom started school and Carrie was trying to darn one of Harry's socks. The girls, who usually sat close together, were either end of the bench. Carrie was getting in a muddle and kept looking at her sister who was ignoring her.

'Louisa, I think Carrie needs some help,' Mary-Ann suggested. Louisa stiffened and pushed her lips together to stop herself answering back.

She looked from the jumble of threads to Carrie's face and suddenly relented. 'I'm sorry little sister,' she said, 'Come on. I'll help.' She smiled at Carrie and patted the bench next to her.

'That's better,' said Mary-Ann as Carrie moved down the bench, 'I don't like to see you two falling out.' The two girls chattered whilst Louisa untangled the darning and by the time Mary-Ann told Carrie to pack away and go to bed half an hour later they were laughing together at Louisa's funny stories about school.

Meanwhile Henry and Thomas had walked some way along the track towards Caister.

'Wind's getting up,' shouted Thomas.

'And it's cold,' replied Henry, 'let's go back. We could go to the King's Arms, it'd be warmer in there.'

'You know I don't drink ale any more. Let's just go home. Before we get there though, there's something I wanted to ask you.' Thomas drew a deep breath. 'Those at the church...'

'You mean your latter-day saints?'

'Yes...er...they've asked us move to America. Apparently the prophet is calling all the pilgrims there.'

'And you want to go?' Thomas nodded so Henry continued, 'you'd be on your own. No family.'

'Yes, but I don't think family will be very good here in a bit. Except for my brother of course.' He turned to Henry, screwing up his eyes as the rain was coming from that direction. 'And I know I'll be leaving you here on your own.' Henry grimaced at the thought because he wouldn't be completely on his own: Edmund would be here. They walked in silence for a while.

'When will you go?'

'They want me on the next sailing in November. Apparently they really need people with my skills.' He paused. 'I wanted to know what you thought.'

'You go Thomas,' replied Henry being careful to keep his voice steady. 'I'll miss you, you know that. But it'll be a good place to have your family. Better than here.' At this point they had arrived home again. Mary-Ann was sitting by the fire and Henry went straight to her.

'Thomas has just told me. They're going to America.'

Mary-Ann's eyes opened wide. 'When?'

'In November.'

Mary-Ann was relieved but Matilda looked startled. 'Didn't you tell him?' she asked. Thomas shook his head.

'Tell me what?' The pitch of Henry's voice had risen.

Matilda turned to Mary-Ann. 'I'm sorry but they want us to move to Liverpool in May. I won't be here for the birth.'

'I'll help in the house,' offered Louisa and her mother gave her a quick smile but then turned back to Matilda.

'But why?'

'They put us all together. All the families,' explained Thomas.

'What do you mean?'

Matilda spoke quietly. 'Apparently there is not much space on the ship so we will be close together – and then travelling across America is hard and takes many weeks. They want to know everyone is sure about going and no-one will make it difficult. That's why they insist we all live together for months before we go. I'm sorry. I wanted to be here for you.'

'I asked whether Matilda could stay here until after the birth and then follow me to Liverpool in August but they said there were no exceptions.'

'That seems unreasonable,' said Henry, his voice showing the agitation he was struggling to control, 'after all, I thought they said families were important.'

'We mustn't stand in their way Henry,' Mary-Ann said, placing her hand on top of his as she did so.

'But…'

'I'm sure mother will come in May when they go,' Mary-Ann continued, 'and after all we have Louisa. She's not a little girl anymore.'

Henry stared into the fire for a long time and then closed his eyes. Abruptly he stood up and went to his own chair. In the silence Mary-Ann looked at him but could think of no words that would help while Louisa studied the shirt cuffs she was sewing. Matilda looked at her husband: he shrugged and shook his head.

7

The following Monday Louisa came home after her first day at the bakers.

'Whatever happened to you?' Harry asked. Eliza started to cry and moved nearer to Tom who just stared.

Louisa laughed. 'It's what they do at the end of your first day. Means that you're OK.' She went out through the kitchen to the back yard.

'She looks like the travelling actors who came at Hallow's Eve,' said Harry.

'You mean like a ghost,' laughed William.

Twenty minutes later when Louisa came back in Carrie had returned from school.

'Was it too horrible?' she asked her. 'The boys told me you came in covered in flour. You still have some in your hair.'

Louisa laughed and then started coughing. It was a few minutes before she could stop.

'It must have got in your lungs,' said Matilda.

Louisa nodded. 'I started coughing when the sack was still over me and Mr Boulter whipped it off.'

'So what happened?' Harry asked. 'Tell us from the beginning.' Just at that moment Henry and Thomas came in but Louisa continued.

'At the end of the day they closed the shop door. Before I knew what was happening someone held my arms and someone else put an empty flour sack over my head. I was told that I would be passed from one person to the next and I had to keep the sack on my head all the time. They'd nearly finished when I started coughing and Mr Boulter took the sack off. They said I'd done well because I didn't take it off myself. Everyone cheered.'

'Well done,' said Henry, 'I'm proud of you. I thought there might be something like that but I didn't tell you.'

'I'm glad you didn't,' said Louisa, rubbing her eyes. 'It would have been worse knowing it was coming.'

'Mmm that smells good,' said Thomas who had caught sight of Matilda piling up fried mackerel on a plate.

'Come on then,' she said, 'hurry up and have your wash and then we can eat. These'll be cold soon.'

'How did you get on today?' Louisa asked Carrie as they settled down with the mending again after dinner.

'I was alright. It's a lot stricter but then we're older so I thought it would be – and I think the teachers speak faster. Mr Blanchard though...' Her voice trailed off while the two girls looked at each other and shuddered.

'He's mean that one,' Louisa explained to the rest of the family. 'What about Miss Rauds? Did she do the object lesson?'

'Yes. It was just a rusty old nail but she made it really interesting. And then we had to draw it but even that was different. Instead of just drawing it on the desk we had to draw it in a new setting – you know imagine it was somewhere else. Jimmy Nudd spoilt it though. He kept nudging the boy next to him. But Miss Raud spotted him and made him stand in the corner.'

'He was lucky he wasn't caned,' suggested Thomas.

'He was!'

'What, on his first day?' Louisa asked.

Carrie nodded. 'Mr Blanchard came into our room and just at that moment Jimmy was turning around pulling faces. He turned back quickly but was seen. Mr Blanchard said, "Miss Rauds, I was coming in to tell you that sounds of the cane might disturb your lesson. But actually," and he looked at Jimmy, "I think some of the younger children need to watch." Then he pulled the partition back. He told us that because two boys had each received three black marks that day they would both have three strokes of the cane on each hand. Then he shouted, "Turn around from the corner boy." Jimmy turned really slowly and stared at Mr Blanchard. "Your first day boy? Well you will have one stroke on each hand so that you learn that here we respect our teachers." He called out the names of two boys and they came forward. You could tell they were scared by the way they walked.'

'Scared,' laughed Harry. 'What's there to be scared about? It stings a bit.' He shrugged. 'I was caned yesterday and today for being late.' At this Henry, who had been rubbing pig's fat into his work boots, looked up sharply.

'Caning at upper school's a hard thing, Harry,' explained Louisa but Harry just grinned and looked at the ceiling.

'Girls,' he whispered to William.

'I didn't like the way Mr Blanchard did it,' said Carrie. 'He didn't just cane one boy and then the other. First, he explained why they received their first black mark. Then he gave the first boy one stroke on each hand and did the same to the second boy. They weren't allowed to rub their hands or anything but had to hold them above their heads so that we could all see the red line. Then he showed Jimmy the cane. It was so much bigger than the lower school one! He told Jimmy that when the boys had received their second strokes it would be Jimmy's turn. Then he explained the second black mark and gave each boy his second stroke. Again they put their hands in the air. Mr Blanchard pointed to the hands and pointed out that the boys had not made a sound when they were hit. He said if Jimmy cried out that hit wouldn't count,' Louisa grimaced, '– and I thought they were just being very brave,' continued Carrie. 'Then Jimmy had his strokes – his face went very red and his hands were shaking when he held them in the air after the hits but he didn't cry. I don't know whether Jimmy's bravery made Mr Blanchard more cross or what, but he told the older boys that their final stroke would teach them a lesson. He had this funny smile and he made them kneel on the floor. He was standing above them and then he really hit them hard. One boy cried out and fell over on the last stroke. We all waited for Mr Blanchard to hit him again but he said that he would do that after morning prayers tomorrow.'

'So now the poor boy has to wait all night for it,' said Matilda, shaking her head.

Then Henry spoke. 'Mr Blanchard sounds very cruel. But on the other hand I don't think lower school is helping you Harry. Go out into the yard and wait for me there.'

'Henry…' Mary-Ann faltered at a look from her husband. The room went quiet as Henry followed his son into the yard. When they returned Henry was fastening his belt whilst Harry, who'd been crying, went straight up to the bedroom.

Half an hour later Louisa put down her mending.

'I can't do any more,' she said, 'my eyes hurt.'

Mary-Ann looked at her. 'They're very red. It must have been the flour. Matilda, could you make some camomile tea?'

'How much?'

'A big pot I think. Louisa needs to drink some.' Louisa pulled a face but her mother continued, 'I know you don't like it but it may soothe your cough especially if we have any honey to go in it. I'd like a cup and make enough for anyone else who wants some. And pour some into a bowl to go cold so that I can bathe Louisa's eyes.' She turned to her husband, 'Henry, where's that new book you brought back from the lending library today?'

'Still in my workbag,' he replied without looking up.

'Perhaps Carrie could have a break from the mending and start it for us.' Carrie smiled with delight. At the sound of his daughter reading, Henry, who had been sitting stiffly on the front edge of his chair, sat back and let the frown on his forehead relax. Mary-Ann smiled for a moment until she remembered her eldest son. She closed her eyes, sipped her tea and hoped he was asleep.

Later that night, in the dark of their room, Henry held Mary-Ann close but he didn't caress her. For a moment Mary-Ann thought he was asleep until he started to speak.

'I needed to punish him. He must have a high regard for those who have authority over him – so that they, in their turn, will know how to be in charge.' In the darkness Mary-Ann did not nod but she squeezed his arm without letting him know her thoughts.

'Are you alright?' Mary-Ann asked Louisa a few mornings later as she came in coughing from the yard.

'Yes Ma,' she replied, coughing again. 'Mrs Boulter says that she was the same when she first started. My eyes are sore and really itchy, especially in the shop when I'm not allowed to rub them. But she says I will get used to the floury air soon.'

Some weeks passed but then Louisa came home in the middle of the day. Mary-Ann and Matilda with Tom and Eliza were sitting at the table eating.

'Louisa home,' called out Tom excitedly. The two adults looked at each other and then at Louisa who looked as if she had been crying.

'I coughed and coughed and coughed. It felt as if I would never stop and then it was hard to breathe. Mrs Boulter sat outside with me.'

'And they've sent you home?' Matilda asked.

'Your eyes are bad,' said Mary-Ann almost at the same time.

'Yes, they've sent me home. Mr Boulter said not to come to the shop – or any bakers and even to go out if you're baking. He said he didn't want to finish me because I was a good worker,' she smiled, 'but I've to stay away from flour until I lose my cough and my eyes are back to normal and then go back. He said he's sure I'll be alright then.'

It was nearly three weeks later that Louisa went back to the bakery. Just after eleven Mr Boulter came through from the bake house at the back and was happy to find her working and well. Louisa afterwards said she remembered that he'd clapped his hands, which were full of flour, and her eyes suddenly itched. Five minutes later she collapsed. Mrs Boulter, and one of Spandler's apprentices who had been sent to the shop for bread, dragged her out onto the street. The apprentice then fetched Henry from the yard.

Mary-Ann jumped up from her chair when Henry burst into the house with Louisa on his back. He laid her on the floor. Louisa had her eyes closed and was sweaty with the effort of breathing. Eliza, who was in the pen, was able to reach her face and started to stroke it, watching her closely. Henry, unable to say or do anything useful, went straight back to work, digging his nails into his palms with anxiety and frustration as he walked.

Mary-Ann went into the kitchen and looked along the shelves. She lifted down one of the earthenware pots but was careful not to remove the lid.

'Matilda,' she said as she hurried back to them. I have put a jar next to the sink and in it you'll find some juniper berries. Use the old mortar and pestle.' Matilda frowned. 'It's under the sink behind the slops bucket – has a crack so I no longer use it for food. Grind up about ten berries then cover them with almost boiling water. Louisa needs to sit up and breathe in the vapours.'

'But…'

'I can't help you. If I breathe it the babies may come.' Matilda looked startled. 'Don't worry, I'm going up for my rest early. Just make sure that the mortar and pestle are outside and the lid is back on the jar and it's back where it belongs – oh and air the house before you send for me to come down.'

Two hours later Louisa was in the bedroom lying down. Mary-Ann had returned to the living area and they were having some bread and cheese.

'Hopefully she'll sleep,' Matilda said, 'she must be exhausted.'

'Ousa?' Eliza asked.

Mary smiled and looked into the eyes of her youngest daughter. 'Louisa will get better,' she said and then to Matilda, 'although it may take a while.'

8

The following day dawned clear, blue and very cold. North Road sloped along its width towards the east and carts, riding the hard, frozen mud, slid towards that side of the road as the horses, blowing huge plumes of steam, endeavoured to pull them south towards the market. Because the main drain was frozen the air was devoid of smell, which was pleasant, but everyone hoped for a quick thaw: if the freeze continued carts would be brought in to be loaded with the waste from the market and drawn along Northgate and up Garrison Walk to the river. They were not watertight and were usually piled too high so that waste fell onto the road: local people preferred to smell the waste rather than walk in it.

'I've decided I'm going to tell Uncle Robert this morning,' said Thomas as he and Henry walked towards the yard.

Henry frowned. 'What do you think he'll say? After all you were his apprentice and he has trained you. I can't see him being very pleased that you're going.'

'Young Oliver learns quickly. I'm going to offer to spend extra time with him. He won't be fully trained by the time I go but, like I say, he's quick.'

'Yes, but I know what Uncle Robert will think,' he glanced at his younger brother, 'you know Oliver won't be able to do what you can.'

Thomas paused at the door to the yard as if considering the problem but then shrugged. 'Even if he doesn't like it I'm still going,' he said to the air, no longer talking to Henry. He turned, pushed the door open and stepped through to the yard leaving Henry standing outside.

'I know you are,' muttered Henry to the closing door.

Later that morning Edmund came over to them. 'What have you done to upset my father? He's really cross but he won't tell me why. Says I've got to find out from you. I've a feeling he thinks it's my fault.'

Henry was crouched next to Bessie, the steam engine, and he replied without moving. 'Does he? What if we don't want to tell you? What if he doesn't want us to tell you?'

Thomas looked from his brother to his cousin. 'You'll know soon enough anyway so I might as well tell you.' Henry shrugged as Thomas continued, 'I'm leaving the yard. In fact, I'm leaving Yarmouth.'

Edmund tittered. 'What you as well? We struggled when the others went.'

'I've not started my family yet so it's a good time to go. After all there's no future here for me,' stated Thomas.

'What do you mean? We need your skills.' Edmund's voice was raised.

'I mean that in the future you're going to be running this yard and I don't want to work for you.' Thomas spoke quietly and without emotion. Edmund's face grew red, his eyes widened and he stared at Thomas before turning on his heels and walking off.

Half way across the yard he turned back. 'Why don't you go too Henry?' he snarled, 'don't need you either.'

'I'm sorry Henry,' said Thomas when Edmund was out of earshot, 'leaving you here with him – and I feel a bit like I'm letting Uncle Robert down.'

'No, Thomas, you're right. There is no future here for you.'

'Even if Uncle Robert changed his will and left the yard to you he would be bound to include Edmund in it. If Edmund died or –'

'Thomas!'

'Well, without him and if Frederick and George came back from London, I'm sure we could build this yard up.'

'Yes, you're probably right, but that's not going to happen,' pointed out Henry, 'but it's interesting that Uncle Robert gave Ed the impression that it was his fault you were leaving.'

'Hey, look out, he's coming back,' called out Thomas, as Edmund came out of the workshop in their direction. The loudness of his voice meant that the apprentices in the yard turned to look. Edmund's whole body wobbled as he stormed across the yard and the apprentices grinned at each other in amusement. One of them had just finished trimming a branch and tossed it towards the pile by a lathe ready for turning. It landed short of the pile at the same time as Edmund, causing him to trip.

Henry chuckled. 'Maybe it might happen.' Thomas grinned but then his face froze as Edmund stood up with a mallet in his hand.

'I'll teach you two to laugh,' Edmund shouted as he approached them, 'you're no good both of you. You'll come back in a few years Thomas – and you won't work here. You'll be ruined then, a failure like your father.'

Henry stood up and turned to face him, clenching his fists.

'Steady Henry,' said Thomas quietly, 'steady. He's just full of wind.'

'Edmund!' Robert bellowed from the door of the workshop. His son ignored him so Robert nodded towards the apprentices. They rushed forward and grabbed Edmund, causing him to fall again.

Robert approached and wrenched the mallet from him. 'Go home,' he spat. Henry let out a long, audible breath. Robert turned to the two brothers. 'I'm going to the cottage before he tells the wrong tale to his mother. Can you bring things back to normal here?' He looked round the yard where no-one was working and, without waiting for a reply, went after his son.

Later that evening Robert and his wife Mary came to Francis buildings. Henry answered the door to them. Nobody smiled. They sat down and Louisa and Carrie served steaming tankards of tea. Robert tasted peppermint and his eyes flicked towards Mary-Ann; she nodded in acknowledgement. The girls, sensing that this might not be the most pleasant of evenings, picked up the mending basket and went through to the kitchen with it.

The two Marys looked at each other. They both knew what had happened at the yard that day and saw the problem. Had they been alone, without their husbands, they may well have voiced solutions; now they smiled at each other, which was all they could do.

'I have no argument with you,' Robert said to Henry. He glanced at Thomas who bristled but remained silent.

'I'm pleased to hear that uncle. I...er...we have always done our best by Spandler's yard.'

'I have come tonight because all that has happened today has brought to the front of my head lots of thoughts that I have had for a while. Not just what you have told me Thomas,' he turned towards him, 'but how my son reacted.'

'He has not come with you?' The tone of Thomas's question betrayed his scorn.

'He collapsed when he reached home. His heart was very fast and he was sweating and sweating,' squeaked Robert's wife. 'The doctor's with him.'

'I fear for the yard,' continued Robert, 'and you know I am not well myself. Thomas, will you not reconsider?'

Thomas stared at his uncle for a few moments until Henry put his hand on his brother's shoulder and spoke for him. 'I can see that the yard will struggle without Thomas – but think on this: Edmund detests us both.' Robert and Mary looked shocked at the bluntness of the statement and Robert looked to be about to object but Henry raised his hand before he continued, 'Thomas is young and newlywed. This is a good time for him to start a new life, although God knows we don't want to see them go. He has no future here.'

'But I will speak with Edmund, when he has recovered of course, and teach him how to work with you. The three of you could make the yard very profitable.'

'And when you've gone, Uncle Robert, what then?' Thomas spoke very quietly. 'Edmund will turn on us and this opportunity I have will have passed. Matilda and I will probably have children of our own by then. No, this is the time to go.'

Robert sagged. 'I fear that no-one will work with Edmund. What about you Henry?'

'Well you surely know that I must stay. I could not go and try to seek a fortune and leave a family behind and you know why,' Robert nodded, 'but I must say though that I also fear as to how the yard will work once Edmund takes over.'

'I have talked about changing my will to leave the yard to you but Mary objects and, after all, he is my son. I won't do that, but even if I did I think he would contest it in the courts. He has so many swaggering lawyer friends.'

'I would try to work with him,' offered Henry but his face betrayed his misgivings.

'I'm going to add a codicil to my will to say that all decisions need to be endorsed by Mary while she is alive. I can do no more than that,' stated Robert. He grimaced and rubbed his belly.

'How do you feel about that?' said Mary-Ann to Mary. 'What will happen when Edmund comes to you saying that he should have his way in some decision that Henry thinks is wrong?'

'I-I don't know,' Robert's wife stuttered, 'how would I know what the right decision was between the two of them?'

'Much as I do not like saying this about my own son, Edmund's ideas will most likely be the wrong ones. He does not seem to have a millwright's mind like the rest of us. He doesn't understand the craft beyond the basic principles although he's served his time and will follow me as the master millwright-in-charge.' Thomas stifled a snort. 'You need to trust Henry's judgement. Will you be able to do that?' He looked at his wife's face. 'I think you need something to give you strength against Edmund. He is your son and it is difficult for you to deny what he wants. Henry, can we use your Bible?' The room went quiet as Henry stood up and lifted the book from the shelf. He passed it to his uncle who placed his wife's hand upon it. It was so quiet that Louisa and Carrie looked in from the kitchen: they stood transfixed as Robert spoke the promise and Mary repeated the words which effectively disempowered her son. The silence stretched and the scene was imprinted in the mind of eleven year old Carrie. From then she had an awe, almost a fear, of the Holy Book: even when she was an old lady, when men were beginning to drive carriages without horses, she would shudder if she had even to touch it. Suddenly Robert slumped in his chair, his face white with pain.

'Louisa, make some more peppermint tea and stir some bicarb into it this time,' ordered Mary-Ann. 'Then make everyone else another drink but do Uncle Robert's first.'

A few minutes later Robert was sipping his tea slowly. 'Thank-you, although I'm not sure if it's my stomach or my heart that is sick. It is difficult to admit that your son does not have your own craft. First Robert went to sea and that was hard. Then Edmund – he must know himself that he hasn't the ability to be master-in-charge but he still wouldn't give way to Richard who is the only one of my sons who has inherited the Spandlers' natural ability – and now Richard's gone to London.' Robert stopped and sighed but then shook his head and continued, 'I miss your father and James. If it hadn't been for Edmund, Frederick and George, James's boys, may have stayed, although what we've done here tonight may yet save the yard.'

'It gives me no pleasure.' Henry stated.

'I wish you well Thomas,' Robert continued. 'you'll make a good life for yourself over there I'm sure. You know that Edmund went a few years ago?' Thomas looked surprised and shook his head. Robert half smiled. 'Before he went he wasn't interested in the yard but when he came back it was different – it was as if he realised how much work was already done for him here. I've tried to train him but he's hard to teach – it's as if he already decides what he will do so he doesn't listen. It's going to be difficult when I've gone Henry. He will find out when my will is read, not before.' Henry nodded.

That night he lay awake for a long time. *Perhaps if Edmund had stayed in America or even had drowned during the crossing? From what Robert said it sounded as if he would be leaving the yard to me – but Edmund s alive, damn him!* Every time Henry closed his eyes he could see him grinning. He pressed his fists into his eyes until he felt as if his eyeballs were about to burst. Eventually he slept.

9

A few weeks later Henry came in from work and sat on the children's bench next to Louisa. Eliza toddled over and he picked her up. He looked at the two of them, one just becoming a girl rather than a baby and the other about to leave her childhood behind. They were his daughters and he loved them – he also had plans for them about which they had no idea. Around the time of William's birth he'd had a dream in which he was leading one of his daughters down the aisle at her wedding. There had been many people there in fine clothes so she must be marrying someone from a well-off family. He could not work out how it would happen because his family would have to advance in order for a daughter could marry well, but he was determined that it would.

'How are you Louisa? I don't think I heard you cough at all last night.'

'I'm better. I was going to go to Palmer's tomorrow and see if they're taking on.' Henry was shaking his head. 'But why not Pa? I've worked in one shop and I know Palmer's is bigger than the bakers but I'm sure selling is the same. Mr Boulter said he would give me a letter to say I was good with the customers.'

'I don't want you to look for another job.'

Louisa looked puzzled. 'I don't understand.'

'I want you to stay at home. After all, Matilda will be going soon.' Eliza stopped playing and watched her father.

Matilda? What does he mean, where is she going? She started to whimper.

Matilda, with Carrie's help, was just preparing tea. 'Go and take Eliza from your father,' she said to her, 'she seems upset and he's trying to talk to Louisa. I can put the food on the plates myself.'

Henry passed Eliza to Carrie who walked over to her father's chair next to Mary-Ann. Eliza, uncharacteristically, kept crying. She was pointing at Matilda.

'Matilda's getting tea ready,' said Mary-Ann, not understanding.

'You have become a very capable young woman,' Henry was telling his eldest daughter. 'I know that you help and that you know a lot about running the house but I think it will be easier for you when you take over if you work together with Matilda for a few weeks.'

'But what about the birth?' asked Louisa, panic in her voice.

'No, I don't expect you to do that. Grandma will come from the farm to help.'

Louisa smiled. 'I'll enjoy working with Matilda for her last few weeks. I'm going to miss her.'

'We all will,' said Henry, his voice raised as he looked over at Matilda who was still whimpering.

Mary-Ann looked up at him, 'We all will what?'

'Miss Matilda when she goes,' said Henry. Eliza was quiet for a moment. Then she cried, loudly.

'Eliza,' called out Mary-Ann above the cries. Eliza returned to whimpering. 'Eliza, what's wrong?' Mary-Ann's voice was quieter now and Eliza leaned her head towards her. Mary-Ann took her onto her lap.'

Eliza looked round the room before pointing towards Matilda. 'Dada,' she cried. Matilda dropped the serving spoon into the pot, took the young girl from her mother and hugged her.

'I don't think she knew that you and Thomas were leaving,' suggested Mary-Ann. Eliza's eyes grew large and she craned her neck round to look at her uncle.

'Tomtom,' she wailed. Matilda could not comfort her and passed her back to her mother. It wasn't until Henry took her that she stopped: he walked up and down with her and she suddenly fell asleep. By this time the meal was ready.

'Put her up in her bed,' Mary-Ann said. 'If she wakes later she can eat then.

'I suppose we've never spoken about it when she's been up,' commented Matilda as they sat down to eat.

'Did you boys know?' Henry asked.

Harry nodded. 'Uncle Tom told us when we all went down to the beach to look for driftwood. One Sunday afternoon I think it was. Pa had said that the wood pile was going down and sent William and me but Tom wanted to go as well – so then Uncle Tom said he would come.'

'I remember that because you brought back so much that we took some next door to Mrs Johnson,' said Matilda.

'We collected more than that,' interjected William, grinning and looking at this uncle. 'We had a fire on the beach and cooked some fish Uncle Tom bought.'

'Yes, I wondered why you weren't asking for food as soon as you returned!'

'We had a really good time,' said Thomas,' and I wanted to remember them all having fun – so we built this fire. A man who'd been out in a small boat fishing had caught so much that he was struggling to carry it and I bought a couple of mackerel from him. I said to them then that we were going.'

'But nobody told Eliza,' said Louisa. 'I suppose we still think of her as the baby, that she wouldn't understand.'

'Well she certainly understood then,' said Matilda, 'I'm going to spend some special Eliza time tomorrow – sing some songs, she likes that – and have a story – and talk with her about it. See if I can make her feel a bit better.'

Thomas and Matilda's departure day arrived. No one spoke at breakfast and they all avoided meeting each other's eyes. Henry, together with Louisa, Carrie, Harry and William, went with them to the railway station but it was decided that Tom and Eliza would stay with Mary-Ann. Mary-Ann said goodbye, forcing a smile and keeping her voice steady. After they'd gone she sat and cried. Eliza climbed onto her knee and cried with her. Tom, although older than Eliza by two years, did not seem to be aware of what was happening.

Great Yarmouth was, of course, the end of the line and when they reached the station the train was already at the platform.

'Oh! Climb on quickly,' panicked Carrie, 'it'll go without you.'

'It's not due to leave for another twenty minutes,' explained Matilda, giving her a hug and the next moment playfully pushing her away. 'Do you want me to go so much?' Carrie shook her head and they hugged again.

Harry kept looking up the platform towards the engine and William couldn't keep still in his excitement. Henry also kept glancing that way.

'Well you can tell whose sons they are,' laughed Thomas and all three of them quickly looked at him. He turned to Matilda,' We're going away and they may never see us again, but they want to see the engine,' he chuckled.

She smiled. 'We could stroll along the platform if you like.' Both boys nodded, their bodies bouncing with their heads. As they walked Matilda, Louisa and Carrie linked arms and were so close that they moved as one person. Louisa was already swallowing hard. The boys approached the engine with some trepidation: it was huge. Henry crouched next to his sons and explained the parts that they could see, their young foreheads frowning with the effort of comprehension. Thomas's eyes were wide as he allowed the image of his brother and nephews maximum access to his brain: it would have to last. Finally, it was time and they turned back to their carriage. During the goodbyes Louisa and Carrie kept their tears in check but by the time the train had disappeared they were both crying.

'Well they've gone,' intoned Henry.

'Gone!' echoed Harry.

'Uncle Tom!' William's voice squeaked with the realisation. Henry walked home slowly, his shoulders hunched. He hoped Tom would arrive in America safely and be happy there and raise a family. Now that he had gone Henry was the only one from his father's family in Yarmouth.

Three days later Mary-Ann woke feeling uncomfortable. As she stood up from her bed liquid flowed down her legs. Her babies were coming. She shivered.

On his way to work Henry posted a note to his mother-in-law, Abigail, which she received at eleven o'clock. At the yard he was able to borrow the cart to fetch her from the farm near Caister where she lived: she was ready when he arrived. It was early evening when he returned to Francis Buildings with her.

'Grandma,' called out William. Tom jumped up and down in excitement and Eliza reached over the top of the pen towards her. Abigail passed Louisa a basket full of produce from the farm.

'Boys, can you take those sacks upstairs?' she asked.

'Put it next t'my bed,' instructed Mary-Ann. Abigail turned towards her and raised her eyebrows questioningly. She shook her head: after the breaking of her waters labour had stalled and she was not having any pains. Abigail gave her a bitter tasting tea which made her sick and also had the effect making her dash to the privy. She'd just returned, and they were in the kitchen talking, when Henry came in from work.

'Henry,' called Abigail. He went through to the kitchen, ignoring Eliza who was crying. 'Take Mary-Ann for a walk up as far as the church and back. As fast as she can manage.' Henry frowned uncomprehendingly. 'The pains haven't started,' Abigail explained, 'they need t'start soon or she'll be dry and the babies'll get stuck. The walk might help.' By the time they returned twenty-five minutes later Abigail had prepared the bed by laying straw underneath the bottom sheet. Mary-Ann was breathless.

'Go upstairs and get in t'bed,' Abigail instructed, 'On yer back as limply as you can.'

Mary-Ann didn't reply. She looked slowly round the room at her family: Louisa and Carrie, her girls, Harry, Will and little Tom and of course her baby Eliza. Henry was watching her; their eyes locked but then she shook herself and went through the door to the stairs.

Ten minutes later Abigail came up to the bedroom with Henry. 'Nothing yet?'

'An ache just after I lay down,' replied Mary-Ann, 'but that's not there now.'

'Henry I want you t'help,' suggested Abigail. He looked surprised. 'I'm goin' back downstairs in a few minutes. I want you t'roll her dugs in yer fingers.' She turned to Mary-Ann. 'For about as long as yew would let a baby feed for. Then stop for as long – oh I

75

suppose as long as yew would wind the baby for. Then do the same with t'other side. Stop if a pain starts. I'm goin' t'help Louisa with tea and get the younger children t'bed. I'll come back then.' She paused. 'It would be good for yew t'spend some time together.' Mary-Ann and Henry looked at each other; they knew what she meant.

The following morning Eliza was distressed. The night had been full of cries and loud voices. Pa, who usually made her laugh, ignored her and went out to the yard. She was unsettled and cried, although she had enough instinct to cry quietly.

Ma, where Ma? Ma gone like Dada?

She sniffed back the tears. Louisa noticed and picked her up. She turned to Carrie who would normally have been at school but who'd been kept at home that morning.

'Poor Eliza, she doesn't understand what's happening,' she said.

'Neither do I,' replied Carrie.

'Ma's giving birth,' Louisa stated keeping her voice level as she wiped Eliza's face: the big brown eyes studied her for a few moments. Then Eliza wriggled and she let her down on the floor.

'Yes, I know that, but it wasn't like this when Eliza was born,' Carrie continued, her face a frown.

'No, but there's two babies this time.'

'Two! Really?'

'Yes, but it's not good. They started to come early – and now it's taking a long time.'

'Will Ma be alright?'

'Maybe,' muttered Louisa her voice now small and strained. They had both heard things that were disconcerting and sat with their own thoughts. A long time passed. Occasionally Abigail would come down. The day wore on.

Harry and William came in from school. William sat on the mat on the floor with his legs stretched out in front of him and Eliza sat on his thigh, happy to have her brothers home: they played on the floor with Tom and the animals that grandfather had whittled out of wood on the farm. Harry sat at the table reading, his hair still sticking up all over the place from when he had taken his cap off.

Abigail came down from the bedroom again. Eliza looked up and decided that while Ma was not there Grandma would do. She toddled over to her expectantly and she was picked up. She babbled but was confused and disappointed because there was no response.

'There's good girls. Keep the little ones quiet.' She kissed Eliza's head and gave her a weary smile before turning back to Louisa and Carrie. 'It's all over,' she stated.

'But we haven't heard the babies cry!' Louisa blurted. Abigail shook her head.

'You won't. They're dead,' she said abruptly. Eliza was studying Grandma's face.

Why did she smile and then stop?

'Ma?' questioned Carrie, fear in her voice.

'She's poorly. Lost a lot of blood. Needs t'rest.' At that moment Henry returned from his work at the yard. He looked at Abigail and went straight up to see Mary-Ann. Abigail followed him.

Carrie burst into tears. 'Poor Ma. All that for nothing.'

'At least she's alive,' retorted Louisa.

'I love Eliza but I don't ever want to have one myself.' Carrie cuddled Eliza fiercely.

'You will, when you're married,' Louisa stated, looking up at her younger sister: that's how it would be – unless she ended up an old maid. Louisa grimaced at the thought.

Upstairs Henry entered the bedroom. Mary-Ann did not move. Her face was grey. Henry stood as if calcified until Abigail touched his arm.

'She's alive but very weak. Don't wake her,' she whispered. She led Henry over to two bundles of cloth on the chest. She had warned him before he left for work that morning but he looked dazed for a moment. Then he looked at Abigail. His hands shook as he unwrapped the two bodies. He held them together: two tiny boys, not much longer than his hands.

'My babies,' called out a thin voice. Abigail put herself between her daughter and the dead children. 'I want to see them,' Mary-Ann insisted, trying to sit up. Her mother went to her side and gently laid her back down.

'Don't Mary-Ann. Don't look. Forget you were ever pregnant.'

'You said that t'me before. A long time ago.' Abigail frowned. 'They're my children Ma. They moved inside me. I cannot forget them. I must see.'

Henry came to the other side of the bed with the bodies; his cheeks were wet. Abigail looked at him and Mary-Ann followed her gaze. She reached out to them.

'They're cold,' Henry warned. 'Just look at them. Two little boys. Remember them warm and alive inside you.'

Mary-Ann drew her hand back. 'They look so perfect, just very small.' She looked at her husband. 'They stopped moving yesterday. They died then. I think I knew. I just ho...' She wept. Abigail hugged her while Henry turned to the chest and wrapped the bodies again.

'Old John died this morning,' Henry said, his back still turned to his wife, 'Someone said his son is there.' Henry stood at the foot of the bed holding the two parcels. 'I'm sure there'll be room in his coffin. I'll take them and ask.'

'Ma, go down to the children.' Abigail hesitated but Mary-Ann continued. 'Talk to them while Henry goes out. I don't want them to ask him what he's carrying.' The tears came again. Abigail did not move. 'Go on Ma.' She brushed the tears away and closed her eyes. 'I'm tired now. I'll sleep.'

Henry returned half an hour later. He'd spoken sternly to himself: had they lived they would have needed a lot of care and feeding them would have weakened Mary-Ann further. He shuddered. She might have – still yet may – die – but they had been his children and he mourned them. As he entered his home Louisa and Carrie looked up from the table where they were chopping onions on a large slab of wood and he noticed the concern in their eyes: they looked from his face to his hands which were empty and he realised that Abigail would have told them where he'd been. The boys were playing as if nothing had happened. He walked through to the kitchen to see Abigail. She was dropping stale bread into a bowl of whisked up eggs. A side of smoked belly bacon, with the eggs, had also been

78

in the basket that Abigail had given to Louisa when she'd arrived from the farm and it was now hanging in the kitchen. She'd rendered down some of the fat from it and it shimmered in the heat.

'Are those onions ready yet?' Abigail called. The girls brought the slab through and scraped the onion into the tray. It sizzled.

'Girls, Ma's very weak,' stated Henry.

Abigail nodded in agreement. 'She will need a lot of care in the next few weeks if she is going t' recover – but I have t'go back t' the farm. This is the busiest time of the year and Grandpa needs me. He will not eat properly, or rest, if I am not there t' put food in front of him. I have t'go back or he will become ill.' She turned to her son-in-law. 'I'm sorry. Mary-Ann's my daughter. I don't want t'leave her but I must go.'

'I-I will help Ma all I can,' stuttered Louisa.

Abigail smiled at her granddaughter. 'I will stay fer two more days and show yew what t'do.' Louisa's face relaxed.

Henry continued, 'Carrie you're not going back to school for a few weeks. Probably not until the tests at the end of term. I need you to help Louisa look after Tom and Eliza. And I need you both to look after your mother.' The two girls looked at each other. 'Come and see Ma now, but not for long,' he continued.

Louisa and Carrie followed their father through to the living room where Louisa picked up Eliza from the pen. She immediately leaned out of Louisa's arms towards Henry, smiling. Perhaps, she thought, if she made him smile things would return to normal? He ignored her. He looked at Louisa and nodded towards the door to the stairs as he picked up Thomas and reached for William's hand; Harry followed him. Louisa, carrying Eliza, with Carrie staying close, entered the bedroom behind her father and brothers. Immediately Eliza chuckled because there was Ma and at that sound Mary-Ann opened her eyes and smiled: the smile was instantly reflected in the faces of the whole family. As they approached the bed Eliza reached out for her mother while Louisa held on to her tightly, unsure what to do.

'Let her sit on the bed next to me but hold on to her so she can't climb on top of me,' Mary-Ann said. Louisa sat down on the chair next to the bed and Mary-Ann put her arm round Eliza, who snuggled close, content: everything was as it should be now that she had Ma. Henry smiled to see some colour returning to his wife's cheeks. For a few minutes Mary-Ann spoke to the girls about the jobs that they'd need to do that evening. Then she closed her eyes and sighed.

'We need to go,' said Henry, 'Ma needs to rest. And Grandma will have tea ready.'

'But Eliza's gone to sleep,' said Carrie.

'I'll stay with her and do that mending Ma mentioned, if you would fetch it for me,' Louisa suggested, '– and save me some food.'

'Thank you,' Mary-Ann said, not opening her eyes, 'it's nice to feel her warmth next to me'. Eliza, oblivious to them all, slept.

An hour later and Louisa had almost finished the patch on Harry's school trousers. Mary-Ann suddenly opened her eyes.

'Fetch Grandma.' Louisa went to pick up Eliza who was awake and stroking her mother's hair. 'No, leave her. Just fetch Grandma.'

Abigail came.

'I'm bleeding again. I can feel it. I suppose – the babies. They would be suckling by now.'

Abigail nodded and pulled back the blanket. 'When did Eliza last suckle?'

'Oh, about last autumn. When I started being sick. I stopped her then.'

'See if she will,' said Abigail, undoing her daughter's top. She turned Eliza round so that she was facing Mary-Ann. The young girl looked up at her mother and then at the nipple where a drop of milk was already forming: this had been Mary-Ann's eighth pregnancy and her breasts produced milk readily.

'Yes Eliza,' Mary-Ann said softly. Eliza hesitated. Mary-Ann had had to be very firm with her to stop her. 'You can now.' Mary-Ann smiled her encouragement. Eliza smiled back before taking the nipple in her mouth and sucking hard. After a few moments Mary-Ann grimaced. Eliza stopped and she put her hand on Mary-Ann's breast, her eyes filling with tears.

'It's alright little one,' Abigail said to her as she massaged Mary-Ann's belly. 'It hurts Ma but it's making her better.' Eliza resumed sucking, more gently now, watching her mother closely. In spite of her pain Mary-Ann smiled back, erasing Eliza's frown. Whilst Eliza was feeding Abigail removed the blood-soaked straw. She put it on the fire before replacing it with fresh and the smell of burning blood puzzled Eliza.

'Ma,' croaked Mary-Ann, 'I need a drink.' Abigail held Mary-Ann and helped her drink. While she was doing this Eliza climbed off the bed and walked to the other side, looking round for the dinner she thought she could smell being cooked. She looked up at Mary-Ann as Abigail laid her back down.

'Help Ma?' she suggested, looking at the other breast.

'Are you still thirsty?' Abigail asked.

'Help Ma,' Eliza repeated. Abigail lifted her up.

Downstairs everyone had finished dinner and the younger children were getting ready for bed so Louisa decided to deal with them first and have her meal later. Henry was very agitated. Louisa began to help Tom who, with his head inside his nightshirt, was trying to find the arm-holes and was walking round in circles: she caught him just as he fell over. She chuckled at the sight of his bewildered, red face when it finally appeared out of the top of the nightshirt. The sound of laughter was too much for Henry. He walked over to Louisa and dragged her to her feet, bringing his face very close to hers and staring into her eyes.

'She's dying upstairs – and you laugh,' he snarled. 'Where's Eliza? You didn't bring her down. Grandma can't look after her and...' His voice tailed off.

'M-Ma told me to leave her,' Louisa stuttered.

'Go and get her!'

Louisa stood still, fear and confusion immobilising her. Henry raised his arm, his hand curling into a fist, but then abruptly turned and left the house. For several moments no-one moved.

'Come on Tom, let's get you to bed,' Louisa said in an unnaturally light voice. Carrie continued to clear up after tea, placing her sister's plate of food on top of a pan of water on the fire although she wasn't sure how hungry she'd be. Harry helped William get ready for bed. There was no more laughter.

Later, after the boys had all gone to bed, Abigail came down and explained what had happened upstairs but then returned. Carrie yawned.

'Are you coming to bed?' she asked Louisa, 'I'm tired.'

'So am I but I'm jittery. Don't think I'd sleep.' Carrie hugged her. 'Think I'm going to give the kitchen floor a scrub – it might make me feel really tired.'

Twenty minutes later Louisa put her bucket of dirty water outside the back door. She walked through from the kitchen, glancing back with satisfaction at the clean floor. Her hand was on the door to the stairs when the front door opened and Henry fell into the house. Louisa couldn't move. He stumbled over to her and pushed her back into the kitchen. She slipped on the wet floor and as she fell he kicked her. Then he fell on top of her. She was winded and unable to stop him from pulling open the front of her dress. He mauled her breasts and then stuffed one in his mouth with one hand as he tried to reach under her skirts with the other.

'No Pa, no,' she squawked. 'It's me, Louisa.' Suddenly he stopped. The sound of her voice had broken through the alcohol to his brain. He gagged and rolled onto the floor vomiting. She forced herself to her feet and went upstairs leaving him lying there.

Carrie was still awake. She asked no questions as Louisa, still in her clothes, crawled, shivering, into bed. She held her close until she cried herself to sleep.

During this time Abigail had been sleeping with Mary-Ann in order to care for her while Henry slept in his chair in the living room. The following morning Louisa crept past him; he was asleep, dried vomit stuck to his clothes. The room smelt foul. She went through to the kitchen and was just finishing clearing up the mess when she sensed that he was at the door.

'You stink,' she said to him without looking up. 'The children will be down soon. Go and clean yourself.' He only needed four steps to walk diagonally across the kitchen to the back door but even they were unsteady.

'After you went out Grandma came down and said that Ma was still bleeding but not as much.' He stood still with his back towards her. She continued, 'Eliza did it. They put her to suck. Grandma said that Eliza being there gave her the idea.'

He opened the door and turned to look at her. She couldn't interpret the look: at first she thought he was trying to say sorry but then realised he was still drunk and barely awake. She didn't care. As soon as her mother was well she would go somewhere else. She could no longer live with the man she knew as her father.

In the privy Henry's flow finished but he did not move for several minutes. He stared at a knot in the wood while his hands remotely buttoned his flies. Slowly he turned to leave. Then suddenly he turned back and thumped the wall with his fist with enough force to cause pain. He despised himself.

10

Four weeks passed, it was now July and an unusual summer gale was blowing. A runner came to the yard from Pike's mill on the Denes. Something had caused the cap to stick so that the wind, in a sudden squall, had managed to get behind the sails: they were turning backwards. Robert, Henry and two of the apprentices ran there, pushing a cart containing a five-foot length of a stout tree trunk, a pulley and some rope. The wind was making the mill vibrate and the wooden mechanism, not designed to run backwards, was creaking and groaning. Inside the mill it was so loud that they had to communicate by signs. They looped the pulley around one of the beams and Robert and Henry climbed the stairs, vibrations causing the steps to move beneath their feet. Robert and Henry had done this before, at other times in other mills, and knew the risk: the whole mill could fly apart at any moment. The apprentices attached the tree trunk to the pulley and raised it high. Watching the spokes carefully the two men swung the trunk backwards and forwards. Robert started to nod in time with the movement and on the sixth nod they both pushed the wood between the spokes, jamming the sails. The whole building shook violently for a few moments; then everything was still and it was quiet enough to hear the four of them exhale.

'I can't believe that he thought that we could just set the mill going again!' exclaimed Henry as they walked away. In the last week Mary-Ann's appetite had returned and the previous evening she'd come downstairs for the first time: the relief made Henry exuberant.

'If he'd locked down the mill earlier he would be able to start it up as soon as the wind died down again. As it is the cogs will need replacing,' replied Robert.

'More work for us,' grinned Henry.

'Robert! Henry!' They had almost reached the yard when they heard this shout behind them. They turned around.

'Freddie!' they both shouted. All three entered the yard.

'Come into the cottage,' suggested Robert, 'Mary will brew some tea.'

'You've come back then?' Robert asked, 'or is this just a visit?'

'No. We're back – moved in not far from you Henry, in Vauxhall Terrace. Been staying in the Anchor last week until I found somewhere. Ruth and the girls are coming tomorrow.' Frederick was a son of James, Robert's brother. After his father died he had gone to London with his mother, brothers and Edmund's younger brother Richard. Henry always remembered him as being half-handsome. One side of his face was very strong but this effect was spoilt by the scar tissue on the other side: hot coals had fallen out of the fire and landed on his face when he was very young. He'd lost his left eye and the wound, as it healed, had pulled up that side of his mouth into a permanent grin. When they were young Henry had been wary of this peculiar-looking cousin. However, when Freddie started at the yard, Henry was given charge of teaching him some of the complicated theory of the millwright's craft and found that his young apprentice was quick witted: he learnt easily and they laughed a lot. As he became an adult they became good friends and Freddie often used to visit Henry and Mary-Ann when they first moved into Francis buildings. Henry hardly noticed the injuries by the time Freddie left in 1850: his character had eclipsed them.

Edmund arrived. 'What's happening here?' He stopped when he saw Freddie.

'I can see how pleased you are to see my pretty face again,' laughed Freddie, the right side of his mouth grinning higher than the scarring on the left. 'Oh dear, I'm sorry,' he continued, 'I hadn't realised something had happened to your face as well. I have to smile all the time and you're unable to smile to welcome me back!' His eyes danced. Edmund looked at his father, unable to think of a reply.

Robert laughed. 'We're pleased to see you Freddie,' he said, staring pointedly at his son. Awkwardly Edmund held out his hand in greeting, smiling with his mouth whilst his forehead continued to frown.

'Good to have you back,' said Henry, for once feeling a little sorry for Edmund and trying to draw the attention away from him. 'Are you coming here to work?'

'Is that possible uncle?' Freddie asked.

'Father?' Edmund bleated.

Robert ignored him. 'I couldn't turn away my brother's son – besides, you still own a share.' Freddie's whole face smiled and Henry realised that the purpose of the visit was to make sure of his employment. Finishing his tea quickly, Freddie stood up.

'I must go now. You all have work to do and I still have to finish some things at the house.'

'As you're on your own why don't you come to us for your evening meal?' suggested Henry. 'I'm sure Louisa will cope.'

'Louisa?' questioned Freddie, half his face suddenly serious. 'What about Mary-Ann?'

'Mary-Ann's very weak. Twins, stillborn.' Henry was very abrupt. Freddie frowned: this had the effect of moving the scar covering his left eye socket onto his forehead which is why he tried not to do it often. Although they tried not to, both Robert and Henry smiled. Edmund sniggered.

'I'm sorry,' said Freddie, smiling back because he couldn't properly look serious.

'They were babies and, although twins would have been nice, I think Mary-Ann is more upset about their deaths now than I am. I was sad then – now I'm just happy that Mary-Ann is alive.' Henry took the stub of a pencil from behind his ear. 'If you call at Francis buildings on your way home then Louisa will know to put more food on. I'll write her a note. She may not know who you are and Mary-Ann could be upstairs sleeping.'

'Then you can fill us in on the rest of their news when you come to work tomorrow,' suggested Robert.

'Why don't you come?' Henry replied, 'but not for tea – we'll try not to talk much while we're eating. Come about half past seven and we should have the younger ones in bed. You as well Ed,' he smiled at Edmund who nodded imperceptibly, 'and bring Mary,' he said to Robert.

'We went to the Great Exhibition several times,' said Freddie later that evening when they were all squeezed into Henry's living room.

'What was it really like?' Edmund asked.

'More amazing than you can imagine,' replied Freddie.

'Is that right?' questioned Robert. 'I always thought the descriptions were probably very exaggerated.' Freddie was shaking his head as he spoke.

'Other people have said that to me. I've read some accounts and they don't tell you how amazing it really is. Imagine St Nicholas' made of glass – but many times bigger.' He looked round the room but they all just looked puzzled. 'It's been built round several trees that were already there.'

'Never!' interrupted Henry. 'Surely it's impossible for a building that big to be made of glass?'

'It's huge,' Freddie continued, 'and as you get near it you can see it sparkling. Do you know it has been called the crystal palace?'

'Really?' said both the Marys together.

'What of the exhibition?' Henry asked.

'Things from all over the world.'

'Yes, yes, but what about the machines?' asked Henry somewhat impatiently. Everyone laughed, but they all wanted to know.

'Well on display were some huge locomotives. But there was also lots of machines that were actually working. I couldn't see the fire or the boiler so I think the steam must have been coming to them through pipes from outside.'

'Imagine having to control that Henry,' suggested Robert.

Henry laughed. 'What of those machines? What did they do?'

'There was a steam hammer that was used to knock poles into solid rock.'

'Why?' asked Carrie.

'They would be used to support something large – a building or a bridge or something.'

'Oh I see,' she replied, 'and I suppose it would be a lot quicker using the machine rather than men?'

Freddie nodded and laughed. 'I can certainly tell you're a Spandler. You understand well, for a girl.' Carrie blushed with pleasure. Freddie continued, 'There was also an envelope-folding machine. It could make thousands of envelopes in an hour starting from sheets of paper and glue – and it only had two boys operating it!'

'How marvellous!' exclaimed Mary-Ann, who was carried along by the excitement; for the first time since the twins she had some colour in her cheeks. 'How old are your children, Freddie? I remember Ruth was pregnant when you left.'

'Well, Hannah is three, four at Christmas and Emily is six months.'

'Looking forward to meeting them,' she replied, 'and seeing Ruth again.' Harry stood up and looked at his father who nodded his permission to speak.

'I wish you had some boys my age,' he said.

Freddie laughed. 'Sorry young man.' Harry turned his mouth down to look sad but he couldn't maintain it and laughed with Freddie.

'What of the others Freddie?' Mary-Ann asked.

Freddie's face clouded over. 'You know mother died?' Everyone nodded.

'James sent a letter,' Henry explained.

'The streets in London are so busy, so many horses and people in a hurry: it's very hard to get across the road – that's how she died. She really enjoyed living there.' He paused. 'George married in April. Jemima. She's already pregnant.'

'James told us about George's wedding although we didn't know about the baby,' said Henry.

'Did James tell you he has a lady?'

'No!'

'Yes. She's called Ann. Getting married next year. Richard's living with Ann's family as well,' he added, looking at Robert. 'Working in metals.' All the men nodded their approval.

Then Freddie thought of something and turned to Harry. 'I've no driftwood yet. Will you come down to the beach with me tomorrow? I'm sure we could bring some back for here as well.'

'Yes,' beamed Harry, dancing up and down with excitement. 'Can Will and Tom come as well? We haven't been since we went with Uncle Tom before he left.'

Freddie danced up and down copying Harry, who went faster; the faster he went so did Freddie until they both fell into a laughing heap on the floor. This unrehearsed comedy act had many in the room holding their sides and wiping their eyes. Even Edmund was grinning.

'I'm so pleased you've come back Freddie,' said Mary, Robert's wife, when she could breathe enough to speak. 'It's time this family had a good chortle.'

'What time are you expecting Ruth tomorrow?' Henry asked.

'I'm meeting them off the London stage. Six in the evening.'

'That's late. She won't want to be cooking then,' responded Mary. 'Bring them to our cottage on the way to your house. I'll have food ready.'

'Are you going to start working the day after?' Robert asked. 'Then I can retire to the office and the paperwork.' Edmund managed to control himself but was not happy: not only was there now another cousin at the yard but he was James's son and Edmund knew that he still owned a share of the yard. As well as that he didn't relish having his father in the office which would mean he would actually have to work all the time.

Freddie, however, grinned. 'Yes sir,' he said.

'Well you can start at Pike's mill with Henry. The damage needs assessing. I'm so pleased. My days of climbing into mills are finished.' Robert relaxed into his chair.

The following day dawned bright and clear. Freddie, after years in London, enjoyed being on the beach: the sight of the upturned boats on the sand, the sound of the gulls and the taste of salt on his lips all made him feel as if he'd been healed of an illness that he didn't know he had. His wife and his pretty girls would be there that evening and he was looking forward to that. Meanwhile he was with Harry, William and Tom. They made their way along the beach where the high winds that had damaged Pike's mill had also created lots of driftwood and they very quickly found as much as they could carry. For a while they sat in the sunshine behind an upturned boat. The boys spoke about uncle Tom and Matilda whom they missed and asked Freddie questions about his face which adults never did; they were curious and he allowed them to touch his scars.

'We're back,' called Harry as he barged in through the back door, having stacked his wood in the shelter next to the privy. He was quickly followed by his two brothers leaving Freddie standing in the yard holding his bundle of wood. Louisa appeared at the back door.

'Are you coming in? The kettle's on.'

'Yes, thank you, but I mustn't stay long. I just need to get some more food in before they arrive,' replied Freddie as he put his bundle down. Louisa led the way through to the living room where Mary-Ann was sitting in her chair and Eliza was playing in the pen near the front door.

'Hello Mary-Ann,' said Freddie, removing his cap as he spoke, 'I trust you're feeling well today.'

'I am Freddie. I did enjoy last night.' She turned towards the kitchen. 'Yes please,' she said to Louisa who was hovering near the door.

'I've just said that I can't stay long,' he said as Louisa came back with the drinks, 'just long enough to finish this.' He grinned as he held up his cup and Mary-Ann smiled back. Just then the front door opened and Carrie entered with bags of shopping.

'There's hot water in the kettle,' Louisa said to Carrie as she took the shopping through to the kitchen.

'I trust the boys have behaved themselves this morning,' Mary-Ann said.

'Yes, it's been fun. We must do things together, the two families, when we've settled in.'

'What about a picnic on the beach?' suggested Carrie who'd just sat down with her tea. 'The men all have Saturday afternoon off at the yard now.'

Mary-Ann laughed, 'That would be fun but when?' Her face dropped. 'I'm not sure whether I could walk that far. I'm still very weak.'

'Ruth's family has a bath-chair for her mother. I could see if we could borrow it,' offered Freddie.

The following afternoon the men were all out at work. It was the summer break from school and ten-year-old Harry had managed to find a day's work as a weeder in the local nursery. Carrie and William, who was six, had gone with him: William would be able to help Carrie empty Harry's weed bucket when it became full. Neither Carrie nor William would be paid but they enabled Harry to cover more ground and earn more.

Ruth, Hannah and Emily came to Francis buildings. Mary-Ann had remembered Ruth's bright red hair but nothing else: she was also covered in freckles, which appeared however hard she tried to keep out of the sun, and she was inclined to chuckle loudly. Mary-Ann smiled at her suitability as Freddie's wife.

Ruth put Hannah in the pen. Tom, who was sulking because he hadn't been allowed to go with the others that morning, ignored her but Eliza stopped what she was doing and stared at this strange girl with bright red hair; she touched the girl's curls and they were springy so she touched them again and giggled. She was surprised when the girl giggled back and touched her own hair.

'Not quite two years between them. Maybe they'll be friends,' suggested Ruth.

'I hope so,' agreed Mary-Ann, as she turned to look at the baby on Ruth's knee. 'Emily's pretty.' She stroked the layer of soft, downy, red hair on her head.

Ruth smiled. 'Hannah was the same at her age. Everybody is always fascinated by red hair. I can remember getting quite cross with people by the time I was ten or eleven.' She grinned. 'And I was always getting caught if I did anything even a little bit naughty – it's the red hair, you're more easily noticed!'

Mary-Ann laughed. She was enjoying Ruth's company. Eliza didn't follow what the adults were saying but she liked the happy sounds that were coming from her mother. Emily went to sleep after she had been fed and Ruth put her back in the pram.

'Did you bring that from London?'

'Yes, Richard made it. Do you know he is a coachmaker?' Mary-Ann nodded. 'It was his apprenticeship piece. It's like a miniature cab. It even has a hood but instead of a place to fit the horses on it has a handle for me to push. When he'd finished his master let him take it away. Hannah had just been born so he gave it to us.' She went over to the pen, picked up Hannah, and brought her over to Mary-Ann. At a nod from her mother, Louisa picked up Eliza and gave her to Ruth.

Eliza looked from this strange lady with her red hair and pale green eyes to her mother. Hannah cried and leant out of Mary-Ann's arms towards Ruth. The two ladies laughed and swapped their girls back. Eliza laughed with them.

On the way down to the beach the following Saturday Hannah and Eliza travelled in the bath chair because Mary-Ann wanted to walk although she was leaning heavily on Henry's arm by the time they reached the shore. Ruth had brought her new folding stool: all the mechanism was made from metal and, before she sat down, Henry looked closely at it. Mary-Ann sat in the bath-chair next to her and the two mothers talked, passing Emily between them during the afternoon. Louisa and Carrie showed Eliza and Hannah how to make pictures in the sand with shells, small pieces of wood and birds' feathers whilst the men and boys played cricket with a piece of driftwood and the ball Henry had made out of the leather from a worn-out pair of boots.

Eventually the match was finished. The boys flopped down on the sand. It was a warm day.

'Anyone for a paddle?' asked Freddie as he took off his shoes.

'Paddle! Paddle!' shouted the boys. Henry stood bemused. He would never have suggested going in the sea.

'Are any of you coming?' called Freddie to the group of women and girls. Louisa looked at Carrie and raised her eyebrows.

Henry frowned. 'Not the girls surely?' he spluttered.

'Why not?' grinned Freddie. 'They'll only be showing an ankle. Hannah stood up and, although she wasn't quite sure what a paddle meant, she could tell by her father's voice that it was going to be fun.

'Well, just the younger ones then,' said Henry reluctantly. Freddie looked at Louisa and Carrie but they shook their heads: they thought the idea odd and not worth an argument with their father.

'Mind you hold their skirts out of the water,' directed Ruth as Freddie walked away with a barefoot Eliza and Hannah. Henry looked flustered and sat down but after a few moments he took off his shoes and followed them. At first Eliza clung onto him as the cold water touched her toes but soon she and Hannah were giggling together as they jumped and splashed.

At the end of the day the two families returned to their homes.

'I like Uncle Freddie,' declared William as they reached the house.

'And me!' shouted Harry and Tom together.

'I like him lots as well,' agreed Henry. He glanced at Mary and was pleased to see how well she looked. 'I'm glad he's come back even if he does have some strange ideas. Walking in the sea! How silly!'

'We could hear you laughing from where we were sitting Pa,' said Louisa.

Henry smiled. 'I must admit it was fun.'

Later Mary-Ann was helping Eliza put her nightclothes on.

'Do you like your new Aunty Ruth then?' she asked.

'Friends like Da,' Eliza replied. Louisa and Carrie, who were sorting out the bags from the picnic, looked at their mother and they all smiled in agreement.

11

Eliza's third birthday came but Louisa didn't share it because Palmer's had taken her on as a floorwalker. Palmer's, originally a small drapers and silk merchant on market place, had expanded into the shops on either side and into other buildings at the back. Louisa, along with the other shop assistants, lived in the attic alongside the stock.

Mary-Ann was thirty-eight and the twins had been her eighth pregnancy in sixteen years. Although still prone to weakness that made her tired she was again caring for her family. Eliza was a happy, though plain, little girl: her hair, thin and black, hung down straight from her head except when it was untidy which was often; her nose was hooked and her chin small and pointed. She had the appearance of a brown-eyed crow. On her birthday she received small gifts that her family had made. Amongst these she particularly liked the tiny doll that William had carved for her out of a piece of wood: he'd been visiting the farm in January and Grandpa and he had made it together during the bad weather. Mary-Ann and Henry watched Eliza's delight and William's pleasure at her joy; in the years to come they sometimes spoke of it.

Two weeks after her birthday it was Easter Sunday and the family went to church as usual. It always filled Eliza with awe as she entered the large parish church of St Nicholas but this feeling was augmented that day with apprehension: now she was old enough to sit in the children's gallery instead of in the pew with Ma and Pa.

'Now make sure you stay there until Harry comes for you,' Mary-Ann warned her. 'You'll come home with the boys today.'

Harry had monitor duties and had arrived earlier with Tom. William held Eliza's hand and as she started to climb the stairs she giggled to herself with excitement and anticipation. In contrast to his sister William was almost pretty: his face was quite feminine with deep blue eyes, long eyelashes and a mole on his left eyelid; his hair was thick with a slight wave that made it bounce as he moved his head. They walked up the steep, spiral steps together, the pretty boy and the plain girl. The walls were shiny with condensation and Eliza reached her hand out, quickly drawing it back when she felt the film of water. By the time they'd reached the top of the stairs she had let go of William's hand and was given a seat a few rows ahead of him. She sat down and looked with fascination at the church because she'd never seen it from up there. She could see the Spandler family sitting in their pew. Ma and Pa, with Louisa and Carrie who were now too old for the children's gallery, looked small and far away: suddenly she felt very alone.

At first all was well but then she felt a puff of air on her neck. She turned and a big boy next to her grinned; she saw his broken tooth and his breath made her draw back. He tried to put his arm round her but she wriggled out of the way; he pulled her close to himself. Eliza was frightened, forgetting William was sitting a few rows back but he noticed what was happening.

'Hey, you,' he whispered, 'leave her alone.' Eliza smiled. She felt safe now.

'No. Shut up,' sneered the boy. He glanced along the row to the adult in charge, but he had not noticed. He started to try to kiss Eliza. She cried. This was too much for William who stood up and the adult turned to look at them.

'He hurt me,' said Eliza, looking at the boy. The adult pulled her out from amongst the children to sit with him. In this position Eliza was not very far from one of the big lights in the church: she'd never been this close, her attention was taken by it and, like the three-year-old she was, she immediately forgot all about the boy and William.

However, for William the situation continued. The boy turned to face him.

'Get you after,' he hissed.

William hadn't thought of himself when he saw Eliza in trouble but now he was frightened. At only seven years old he had good reason to be: the boy was eleven, tall for his age, with muscles developed from early mornings humping baskets of fish. The service came to an end. Fear prevented William thinking properly. Instead of waiting for Harry, he ran off.

Henry and Harry spent the whole of that day looking for him and Freddie joined in as soon as he heard what had happened. Night was falling by the time they returned. Mary-Ann looked up.

'We'll look again at first light, before work,' Henry uttered with a heavy sigh. Mary-Ann just nodded mutely.

'I'll be back in the morning,' said Freddie: the big, jolly man was unusually serious.

'Has he gone home with one of his friends?' Tom suggested. 'I was with Harry and didn't see him. Come to think of it, I didn't see Nutty, Will's friend, either. He doesn't live far off.'

'Who's Nutty?' Henry asked.

'John Knutt, lives above the bakery on the corner of Row Three.'

'Big boy. Hurt me,' said Eliza. Everyone looked at her. 'Will said stop. At church, big boy hurt me.'

'Who? John Knutt?' asked Henry.

'No, won't be Nutty. He's good,' Tom answered. 'Might know suffin' though.'

'Something,' corrected Henry and Mary-Ann gave him an irritated look. Usually she was quite pleased that Henry liked the children to talk properly, but now it just annoyed her.

'Let's go to his house. Ask him,' said Harry.

'Not all of us,' said Henry, 'Tom, while you know him, you come with me.' Tom was ready almost before Henry had finished speaking. He'd not been included in the search during the day but had been left behind with the women and was pleased to be doing something more than just, 'helping Ma and looking after the girls,' as Henry had said.

John Knutt had seen what had happened in the gallery but didn't know the boy involved, so Henry, still accompanied by Tom, had gone to the house of Mr Jackson, the children's gallery supervisor. On hearing what had happened, he, although having only just returned from evening service, at once led them to the home of the boy. The boy lived in a house in a small alley near Rainbow

Corner. It was dark. Tom stayed close to the adults as they walked down Row Five towards the house, trying hard not to step in the open drain running down the middle of the row. Mr Jackson hammered hard on the front door and it was opened by a tall, gaunt woman with many children milling round her. Her eyes opened wide when she saw them all standing there.

'It's about your Johnny,' Mr Jackson explained, 'is he there?'

'What if he is? What's he done?'

'A young boy has gone missing and John Knutt heard your Johnny threaten him.'

'Dunno nuffin',' said Johnny who'd stood up and was standing behind his mother. 'He ran off ar'er church. Too quick fer me an'orl. Gorn down towards the docks an' I lost him. Heard he wuz missin'. Thought you might come but I dunnow nuffin'.' He looked from Mr Jackson to Henry, fear in his eyes.

'Right young Johnny. I believe you.'

'What? Are you sure?' Henry asked him.

'Yes. I think, knowing Johnny, if he'd caught him William might well have turned up at home with his face thumped and his clothes ripped but he wouldn't have completely disappeared. If he's gone down to the docks he'll be in real danger.'

Four days later there was a knock at the door and Mary-Ann answered it. A man stood there with what she first thought was a bundle of rags.

'Here Missus, you lookin' fer a lost boy?' Mary-Ann's hand flew to her mouth briefly before she opened her arms for her son: she immediately noticed that he was hot with fever. 'Fink he's still breathin',' said the man.

'Th-thank-you,' she stammered.

'Found him in Red Lion alley, down by the quay. There was a ship in – right bad lot, didn't seem to be tradin', more like thievin'. Fink they had him and left him in the alley afore they sailed.'

'Will you tell my husband? Spandler's yard?' The man frowned. Mary-Ann inclined her head up Caister Road towards Northgate. 'Just before you get to the churchyard near the King's Arms?'

The man smiled slightly and nodded. 'Sorry this happen o' kind folks like yew is,' he said, and at that Mary-Ann recognised him as the neighbour of the family she had visited recently; she smiled briefly.

William didn't make a sound as Mary-Ann laid him down and started to remove the rags: she would have been happier if he'd moaned or cried. The right side of his face was badly grazed and swollen, the eye on that side black and puffy and there was a deep gash on his chin but these were nothing to what Mary-Ann found as she removed the rags: there was dried blood, mixed with dirt caked all down his legs and his genitals were swollen, with lesions which were already smelling and leaking pus. She knew, without a doubt, what had happened to him; she also knew that he would probably never father any children. As she was trying to wash away the blood she was aware that Eliza was next to her, patting her back gently: this was something that Mary-Ann herself did to all her children when they were upset. She looked at Eliza: tears were flowing down the little girl's cheeks.

'Will hurt, Ma?' she asked sniffing.

'Yes 'Liza. He's very poorly.'

'Make him better?'

'If we can. Must get a message to Grandma. She'll know. First I need to clean this. When we were children she always made sure our cuts were clean, especially if we'd fallen in the muck.' All the time Mary-Ann cleaned up William, Eliza stood by, holding a bowl of water for Mary-Ann to dip the cloths in and watching her brother intently. He did not move or make a sound.

Henry arrived just as Mary-Ann finished and went straight to his son. Mary-Ann folded the bedclothes back and Henry gasped with horror.

'Can you see if Ma can come?' Mary-Ann asked. Henry nodded.

'When Robert heard what had happened, he told me to go. Doesn't need me back until next week. Here –,' Henry gave Mary-Ann a small bag, heavy with pennies, 'the men said if there's anything we need that they can help with.' Mary-Ann, who had been controlled all the time she was caring for William, now began to cry. Henry took her into his arms and she was immediately aware of the sweaty, metallic smell that she associated with her husband at work.

'Why did this have to happen to Will of all the boys? He's the quiet, gentle one,' she sobbed. Henry could not reply but just hugged her closer. Finally, he let go.

'I'll have to go now, to fetch your Ma.' he said.

'You need food,' she replied, pushing some bread and cheese at him. He was eating it as he went through the door. He set off along the road in the direction of Caister. He walked briskly because he needed to get there as quickly as possible, the ensuing breathlessness helping to dissipate his anxiety. In his mind he could still see the bloodied body of his son and his arm and fist muscles tensed in response to the image.

'Hello there!' a voice called out as a cart passed close by him and then stopped. He drew level with it and the voice continued, 'Do you want a ride? I'm a goin' to Caister.' Henry climbed up next to the carter.

'Thank-you for being so kind,' he said. The man looked closely at Henry.

'Where are you going to in such a hurry this sunny afternoon?'

'To my wife's mother,' replied Henry and went on to explain. As he listened the carter flicked the reins to take his horse up to a canter. Before long they reached the track for the farm and Henry gave his thanks and took his leave. As he walked up the track he wondered, not for the first time, about God's handling of the world: given that there are good and evil people in the world why did God send the evil one to his son and the good one to himself? He raised his fist to the sky.

Six hours had gone by and William had neither opened his eyes nor uttered a sound. Mary-Ann was again bathing his wounds when Robert and Freddie arrived. Carrie let them in and they went straight over to Mary-Ann. Both of them shook their heads when they saw William.

'Men are so evil!' burst out Robert. A tear escaped from Freddie's good eye.

Mary-Ann nodded sadly. 'I'm worried because he doesn't open his eyes or even moan when I clean him.'

'I didn't, Mary-Ann,' Freddie touched his fingers to his face, 'for the first few days. And then I was angry because it hurt so much.'

'Where's Henry?' asked Robert, looking round.

'Gone to fetch my Ma,' replied Mary-Ann.

'Why didn't he come to the yard? I'd have loaned him the cart.'

'He thought that by the time he walked up to the yard – and then you might not have been in. He just set off along the road.'

'Well I'll ride up towards Caister tomorrow and see if I can see them coming back,' offered Robert.

'And if there's anything we can do. Ruth would have the younger two if you need.'

'Thank you both. Would you like tea? Carrie will put the kettle on.'

'No we'd best be getting back,' said Robert. 'I'm sure Mary and Ruth will call in and help when they can.'

'Where's Ma?' Mary-Ann asked the following day when Henry returned.

'Very busy on the farm, but she sent me with these,' he replied taking many jars and pots out of his bag. Abigail, Mary-Ann's mother, had a small herb plot near the cottage on the farm and made creams and potions that often helped when folks were sick. She'd made Henry repeat the instructions for use many times so she knew he understood them, then she let him return so that now he was able to explain them all to Mary-Ann.

However, in spite of Mary-Ann's efforts, the infection became worse and fever set in. William became delirious, alternating between silence and screams. Sometimes he cried out, 'No! No!' Other times he screeched as if in terror, his eyes tightly shut: Mary-Ann would stroke his head and talk softly to him until he became quiet and then he would open his eyes, reach up and touch her face. Eventually he improved: Mary-Ann took it as a good sign when he cried while she cleaned him and he spent a lot of time asleep which she knew would help. Eliza fretted because of her brother and would frequently stop what she was doing and go to his side and watch him: on one of those occasions he opened his eyes. Suddenly his face changed into one of rage and hate far beyond a boy of seven. Eliza recoiled with fright.

'Ma!' Mary-Ann came but by the time she looked over Eliza's shoulder his expression had faded as he again lost consciousness. 'He looked at me. Not Will. Cross,' Eliza said, her face showing her shock and fear.

'He's probably hurting a lot,' Mary-Ann explained. Eliza wandered back to her doll, the one that William had given her only a few weeks before. She remembered the fun they had together before he was hurt and hoped he would be better soon.

Weeks went by and William continued to make progress. He was out of immediate danger but struggled to speak: the only sound that he made, beyond moaning or crying, was to hiss if Eliza came near him. During this time Eliza often stopped with Freddie and Ruth. Although it was always fun at their house and she enjoyed playing with Hannah, Eliza was uneasy. She couldn't understand why her brother didn't like her anymore and knew that he was the reason she was not at home. Mary-Ann didn't know what to say so she just told Eliza not to worry about it. Eliza was confused and sad.

Freddie often came to visit. He would sit with the hurting little boy and, when he was awake, would lift his hands to his own scars. He said nothing to him but would just sit. Strangely, when he was there, William would allow Eliza to stand next to him without reacting.

'He's going away,' said Mary-Ann one evening when Freddie was there. He noticed William flinch even though his eyes were shut. 'He frightens me, with Eliza,' continued Mary-Ann. William snarled silently.

'Don't do that. Eliza's welcome at our house,' suggested Freddie. 'He needs to be with his family.'

Mary-Ann nodded. 'I know but William usually enjoys it at the farm. He can spend the summer there. Then maybe he'll forget.'

Freddie shook his head. 'Mary-Ann, he won't ever do that.'

Abigail arrived and after a few days the decision was made that William would go back with her, away from Yarmouth – and away from Eliza. Mary-Ann had told Henry what Freddie had said but they still decided he should go.

The day arrived for Abigail to return home with her grandson. As she and Mary-Ann bustled round packing a bag for William, he just sat staring at the floor. Then, when they were going, Eliza leaned over to hug him. He grimaced and tried to say something. Her eyes widened. He bit her nose, hard, grabbing huge handfuls of her hair and pulling her head from side to side. She screamed, the pain making her eyes water, her vision blurring. Mary-Ann tried to pull her away but William would not let go until Henry hit his hands hard with the poker from next to the fire. William then turned on his father, hissing and snarling.

'Stop it, Will!' Henry shouted, dropping the poker and holding onto him tightly. Suddenly William flopped into a sullen weight in Henry's arms. He lifted his head and looked around the room: Tom, wide-eyed, shocked and still; Grandma with her coat and bags by the door; the fire burning in the hearth, unconcerned and normal; the water jug by the front door awaiting filling as usual and Eliza, crying and pale, held tightly by Ma, a cloth at her bloody nose. At first he started to hiss as before but then he found his voice.

'I h-hate you,' he said. Although his voice was quiet it had an edge of menace. Eliza shrank back into her mother's arms. 'You!' He stared at Eliza, his lips curling into a snarl. Suddenly, wrenching himself free of Henry, he pulled down his trousers showing his wounds, red, shiny and still healing. 'Yes, h-hold her, p-protect her,' he continued, pointing at Eliza, his voice getting louder. 'But send m-me away.' He spat.

Abigail stepped forward and gently pulled his trousers back up again. Then she held his face in her hands, turning his head so that he could see only her. He started to cry.

'Come now Will, come home with me. Grandpa's waiting for you.' William leaned against her as they walked out of the house and climbed into the cart.

Eliza, bewildered and uncomprehending, cried herself to sleep that night.

William returned at the end of the summer. He'd grown taller and was tanned from working outside on the farm. At first he appeared to be as he was before he was hurt: he was quiet like he'd always been; he'd stopped screaming and no longer reacted violently to Eliza. When he'd returned he even brought her another carved wooden doll for her. However, Eliza was wary of him. Sometimes she would feel odd and look up to find him staring at her when his eyes would narrow and his mouth open to show his teeth. He would often go out on his own: at first Harry would offer to go with him but he always said no. Mary-Ann was unhappy at this but Henry had said that it was good because it meant that he wasn't frightened on his own. One day Harry followed him down to the shore. William was sitting so still near the water that eventually some birds, feeding in the sand left by the receding sea, wandered near to him. Suddenly he moved and the birds took off, except a small long-legged one which had been stunned by a stone. Harry watched and shivered: William skilfully held the bird breast side down on the sand in such a way that the bird, however hard it struggled, could not reach him with its long beak. Then he caught one flapping wing in his other hand and slowly twisted it, his face contorting as he did so. The bird squawked and kicked helplessly. Eventually the wing broke. William removed the second wing in the same way. After that he set the bird on its feet and let go. It tried to scurry away and William, with great glee, raced after it and kicked it into the air. It fell on the sand and tried to run but again and again he kicked it until eventually it could run no longer and he kicked it into the sea. William leapt up and down victoriously but then suddenly flopped to the ground and rolled into a ball with his arms over his head, rocking himself. Harry crept away; he didn't understand what his brother had become.

After he left the shore and turned into St Nicholas Road Harry walked briskly. He had hoped to be at Spandlers' yard in time to meet his father but as he neared the east side of the graveyard the road was suddenly thronged with many people and he realised that, as the silkworks had finished for the day, Henry would be already walking along Caister Road. He knew that he would not catch up with him however fast he walked. Tomorrow he would ask his mother if he could go and meet him from work and he would tell him then.

'Hello Harry,' said Henry as he left the yard the following evening. Son and father turned towards home and walked together along Caister Road.

'Pa, yesterday I followed Will when he went out.' Harry stopped.

'And?' Henry turned and their eyes met briefly. They continued to walk in silence for a few moments before Harry explained what he had seen the previous evening. As he talked Henry's heart thumped inside him.

'Are you sure it was Will?' Henry asked when he had finished. Harry nodded. 'Did he perhaps walk through a group of people and you started following the wrong person?'

'No, Pa, it was Will. I watched him on the shore for a long time. I could tell it was him by the way he moved.'

'Did he see you?'

'No, I don't think so. He's not said anything if he did.'

'What about Ma? have you told her?'

'No.'

'Say nothing. She'll worry.' Henry looked at the frown on his eldest son's face. 'He'll settle down as time passes and he forgets what happened to him.'

'Yes Pa,' replied Harry as they reached the house. He didn't see his father's clenched fists or notice anything amiss in his forced gaiety as he greeted his children.

Mary-Ann noticed that William didn't smile very much and she found it upsetting that he didn't want to cuddle any more. Watching him she sometimes felt as if he was trying to be gentle, but he was jerky as if he'd become a puppet. Occasionally he would do things to hurt or upset Eliza and would look around the room with a strange smile on his face as if to challenge someone to suggest he did it on purpose. She also spoke to Henry who said he was just a boy that he had been made to be older than he was. Henry didn't know what to do. During this time Freddie befriended William and they seemed to be able to talk together: usually William hardly spoke. This disturbed

Henry who was acutely aware that another man was helping his son when he himself could not.

Harry had noticed that whenever Freddie visited William would go to him and one evening, without telling his parents, he went to Freddie's house.

'I'm sorry. I don't know whether I should have come,' he said to Freddie and Ruth's surprised faces at the door, 'but I want to speak to you. It's about William.'

'Come in young Harry. You're always welcome,' said Ruth, 'would you like tea?'

He shook his head. 'It seems strange to be here on my own.'

'That's fine,' said Freddie, 'you're growing up now. What did you want to tell me?'

Harry went on to describe what he'd seen William do on the beach.

'I've told Pa but he suggested it wasn't William but I know that it was. He also told me not to tell Ma so I don't think he would be very happy if he knew I'd told you. He said Will would forget what happened to him in time.'

Freddie didn't comment on this. 'You have to remember that William's been hurt by somebody and, sometimes, when you've been hurt it makes you want to hurt.'

Harry nodded. 'I just thought you would be a good person to tell. I'd best be going home now. Thank you, Uncle Freddie.

During that winter Freddie often took William down to the shore. He had a telescope and they watched the boats together. He also knew the names of many of the sea-birds and talked about them and let him watch them pulling small eels from the sand.

By the following spring William was talking more and would even occasionally sit next to his mother and lean towards her. Then his grandmother Abigail was killed in an accident with a new steam-driven seed drill on the farm and suddenly William reverted to hissing at Eliza. After the funeral at the village church near the farm he locked his arms round the farm gate and refused to go back to Yarmouth. He spent another summer helping his grandfather, by the end of which it was nearly eighteen months since his assault: he appeared to be a normal eight-year-old boy. However he would not allow Eliza to touch him. He shrugged her off or pushed her away if she tried. She was only young; she didn't understand and it made her cry. Occasionally Freddie would be there when this happened and he tried to help by sitting on one side of William whilst Eliza sat on the other: more than the other adults in William's life Freddie understood his anguish and he could empathise with Eliza. Freddie remembered the time after his accident. He knew he'd nearly lost himself in bitterness as he grew up and how it had affected his relationship with his eldest sister: he feared for the two bewildered children.

Henry was glad of his cousin's help although he felt cut off from his son and this exposed his past: he could only see William as yet another failure to add to the deaths of his siblings. When he was eighteen, and his father went to London to try and make his fortune, he had given him charge of his family. Although he had done his best, many of his siblings died, and Henry was left with guilt and nightmares. He had had years of happiness with Mary-Ann but then his brother Tom had left for America, leaving him alone of his father's children in Yarmouth and, since William had been assaulted, he had begun to despair again. He often came home late from work. Mary could smell alcohol although Henry said he'd only been talking things through with Robert over a tankard. She was disturbed because Henry was changing. He didn't talk to her much. In bed he no longer cuddled and caressed: it felt to her as if she was there to satisfy his needs and nothing more. William's hurt had affected them all.

12

Two years passed. It was now almost three and a half years since William had been hurt and he seemed to be completely recovered. Recently, however, he had moved into the senior school and being with the older boys had made him anxious: consequently at home he was unpleasantly rough with Eliza which perplexed her. However most of the time his interactions with his family had become like any other ten-year-old – although Eliza knew he was not the same as Harry and Tom.

At the yard Henry and Robert talked over the day each evening with Edmund sulking in the background as he sat working at the ledgers. Sometimes Robert would come to a site to see the men at work but it was clear to Henry that Robert was becoming frail as he lost more and more weight. Occasionally Edmund would come with him and it was during those years, whilst Henry took on more and more of the running of the yard, that he realised that Edmund was not just lazy: his lips were usually a dusky purple colour and he became breathless very easily. Henry confided in no-one, but he nurtured a hope that Edmund would pre-decease his father.

The year was 1857 and it was harvest time. After the service at St Nicholas's the whole family came to the yard for a meal. This included Elizabeth, Robert and Mary's daughter, with her second husband Robert Flowers whom she'd married in London after her first husband died: they had moved to Yarmouth in June of that year with their eight-year-old daughter Susan.

Mary served a huge leg of pork. Before she'd left for church she'd set it on a vertical spit in front of the furnace in the yard. The spit had been made by Thomas, Henry's brother, before he left for America, and was his gift to Robert and Mary. Once fully wound it took two hours to unwind. He'd designed it to be used specifically with the furnace and it not only rotated the meat but also moved it up and down past the open fire door. In front of the meat and hiding it from view was a tall, curved, metal plate which reflected the fire back onto the meat. When they entered the yard the smell of the pork delighted everyone. Thirty minutes earlier the leg had been removed, taken to the kitchen for carving and replaced by four narrow, cylindrical cages full of large potatoes: each cage had a door which, when closed, spiked the potatoes. The gearing on the spit was altered so that all four cages were rotating individually close to the fire: the reflector plate was put back into position. Half an hour after they arrived back from church the skins were crisp and the potatoes' insides were soft; the cages were opened and the potatoes pulled off the spikes into bowls on the long tables set out in the yard. These were interspersed with platters of roast pork and bowls of steaming vegetables. Everyone sat down to the feast. There was a special table for the children at the side of the cottage, apart from the adults, where Eliza sat with William and Tom as well as her cousins Hannah, Emily and Susan, overseen by Carrie and Louisa. Harry, who had recently started work, sat with the adults.

Twenty minutes went by: there was much chewing and plenty of wiping of greasy chins but not much talking. Then Robert, who had a liking for crackling, began to cough. Someone slapped him on the back and the coughing stopped. He picked up another piece. Mary, his wife, caught his eye and shook her head: over the last few years Robert's problems with his stomach had been getting worse and she was trying to suggest he'd eaten enough for that day. He shrugged and popped it in his mouth. He found that this piece was more leathery than crunchy but there was still a fair amount of fat on it and he enjoyed sucking that off. He chewed at the rind for a while and then swallowed. He coughed. His eyes widened. He tried to cough a second time but he couldn't inhale: his breath sounded like a stiff door being pushed shut. Initially his face had gone red but now his lips were turning blue. Someone slapped his back again. Mary screamed. Henry, Freddie and Robert Flowers, quickly grasping what was happening, lifted him and turned him upside-down. Edmund thumped his back. A ball of chewed pork rind flew out of his mouth. They laid him on the floor. Everyone was still and quiet, the only sound being the chatter of the children who were out of sight. Robert's face was now pale except for the area round his nose and mouth which was a dusky purple. Gradually the purple faded but he did not open his eyes. Someone put a mirror to his mouth and it misted and at that moment the doctor appeared. He ordered him to be carried to bed where he applied leaches to his throat to draw off the congestion. The following morning, however, he was dead.

After Robert's death the millwright business was suspended except that Henry went out to a broken pump that they had promised to repair the previous week. It was not a difficult job and he worked automatically, his mind numb. He wanted to cry and the suppressed tears were acidic with bitterness: there was sadness at the loss of his uncle but mainly it was the loss of his secret hope, replaced by angry despair. Although it was only mid-day he called in at the pub on the way home. In the time it took him to drink a pint no fewer than six people came up to him to offer their condolences. He was struggling to control himself and so bought a flagon of ale and took it home with him. Mary-Ann protested but he turned his chair to face the wall and drank it all. It exacerbated his sadness and he cried. Hesitatingly Mary-Ann approached the chair from the side; he held out a hand towards her and she went to him. She held his head in her hands until he stopped crying and sleep overcame him.

In Spandler's yard the building containing the office also had a large room where wood and iron, the raw materials of the millwright's craft, were stored. The storeroom and its contents were now covered with large black sheets and it was here that the coffin lay with its lid not yet fixed so that, if he were not truly dead, Robert could save himself. The room was filled with what flowers could be found in October supplemented by burners filled with scented oil. The sight was impressive even if, as the days passed, the odour of death bore witness to its certainty. Many people in the area of Northgate came to pay their respects. Mary and Edmund stayed in the cottage behind closed curtains until nightfall when the door to the yard was closed and the family gathered round the coffin. Henry and Freddie and their families, together with Aunt Hannah, Robert's sister, would stay for a few hours each evening until they went home and left Mary with Edmund and his sisters Susanna, Elizabeth and Martha to watch through the night. Word had been sent to Richard in London and it was hoped that he would return before the funeral. The eldest son, Robert, was a seaman and there was no way of contacting him, so it was a surprise when, on the third evening, he walked in.

'Why are you here?' asked Edmund the suddenness of it making him abrupt.

'Edmund,' admonished his mother from under her black veil, 'you were not the only son remember.' Edmund's eyes narrowed and, although he did not repeat the question, his face challenged Robert for an answer.

'We just happened to have reached here now. I'm just sad that the winds weren't better. Then I might have seen him alive.' He looked at Edmund. 'It's alright Ed. I don't want the yard. Father helped me buy my share of the boat. I don't want any more.'

'I didn't know that.' Edmund's voice squeaked.

'What?' Robert was puzzled.

'That father helped you buy into the boat.' Edmund sneered. 'You weren't even prepared to wait until he was dead to ask for money.'

'Father suggested it. You ought to be glad. It means I'm not a millwright and I'm not interested in the yard.' Edmund scowled but Robert ignored him. He approached Mary and went to take hold of her hands.

'I can't see you,' she said, pulling one hand away and lifting her veil. 'That's better.'

'Mother.' Edmund's voice was raised. 'You are in mourning. You must not be seen without your veil.'

'Leave mother be,' ordered Robert, his voice cracking. He was used to giving orders on the boat but this was different.

'We are all family here,' added Henry, 'the veil is unnecessary.' Edmund scowled and looked at the floor.

Ignoring them all Mary asked her eldest son, 'Robert, how long are you here for?'

'Three weeks. They will sail to Newcastle without me tomorrow. That had been arranged before I knew.'

Mary smiled as her eyes simultaneously filled with tears. 'All I need is for Richard to arrive and all my boys will be here.'

'Richard? Oh, and I suppose father gave money to him when he left as well?' Edmund provoked. They were all shocked into silence by his hard-heartedness.

Mary pulled down her veil to hide her face from Edmund's glare. 'I do not know,' she said, sadly. After the funeral her husband's will would be read and she was not looking forward to it.

Eliza was standing waiting for the procession to move. At six and a half she was expected to take her place with the older children of the family who would all walk immediately behind the coffin. She was the first child in the procession, being the youngest of her generation who was old enough to walk separately from her mother. Behind her were Hannah and Susan and the boys followed by the younger children with their mothers and other women who grouped themselves around Mary, Robert's widow, to support her. Eliza looked round enviously at Emily. Her left arm was already sore from being rubbed by the roughly finished seam of the new, long, black dress she was wearing. She had tried to ease it but the thickness of her white gloves made it impossible and Louisa had frowned at her wriggling and shook her head slightly. She had nothing to do while she waited for the procession to move but she didn't dare turn around and talk to Hannah because too many adults were watching and one of them would be bound to tell her father. Her attention was caught by the flintstones in between the bricks on the wall of the yard: it formed a pattern, brick, stone, brick stone in each row with the rows arranged so that underneath each brick was a stone. Just when she thought they were ready to go another adult would move. They looked, to her eyes, strangely smart and serious as they fussed about where they should be in the procession. Even Freddie did not return her smile when he passed her on his way to join the men who were in the room where Robert's coffin was now being sealed. A few moments later she watched her father and the other the men manoeuvre the coffin out of the building and lift it onto their shoulders. She knew that people died because one of her friends was no longer coming to school and the teacher had told them that she had died. Old Uncle Robert had died and was in that box called a coffin but she wondered if he could see in there and what he would eat when he became hungry. Now they were all walking round the edge of the graveyard to the church; she tried to walk without moving her arm as much as possible. She stood still in the church during the service although at one point she was leaning against Louisa because it took a long time as one person after another spoke about Uncle Robert: she wondered whether he could hear in the box and if he couldn't why they were saying it all. The service ended and the men picked up the coffin again and they left the church, followed by the women. Eliza wondered where they were going but together with the other children she was taken back to the cottage.

'Louisa where have they taken Uncle Robert?' she asked as they walked.

'To bury him of course,' Louisa replied. She smiled when she saw Eliza's puzzled face. 'The gravediggers have dug a hole in the ground. The coffin has Uncle Robert's body in it.' She looked at Eliza who nodded. She understood that much. 'It will be lowered into the ground and then covered over with earth. That's what burying means, it's what we do at a funeral,' she explained.

Then Eliza looked shocked. 'But how will he get out?' she asked.

'He's dead Eliza. He can't get out. He can't move. He's dead,' she repeated.

Eliza's eyes opened wide as she grappled with understanding. 'But you mean we won't see him anymore?'

Louisa shook her head and replied in a quiet voice, 'No-one will, not even Aunty Mary.' Eliza fell silent: now she understood why Uncle Freddie hadn't smiled at her and everyone was looking so sad. Her friend from school must be under the ground with the earth on top of her. She shuddered.

When the children arrived at the yard they were greeted by John Riches, the publican from the King's Arms next door. His face was serious as he took off his cap. In the absence of any of the older women he came over to Louisa. From where she was standing Eliza was able to look up one of his large nostrils whilst he spoke with Louisa: she was amazed at the long black hairs that protruded from it. Her older brothers helped to put tables out in the yard and when they had finished staff from the King's Arms brought out food. The last space was just being filled on the tables as the adults arrived. People began to help themselves to food and Eliza was pleased to see that some of them now smiled a little.

'Richard!' Eliza looked up at the shout. Everyone was looking at a young man, dressed in a dark suit and carrying a top hat, who had just entered the yard.

'One of the horses on the coach lost a shoe and we had to call in at Ipswich,' he said in a voice that was surprisingly loud and deep for such a slight young man.

'You're here now,' called out his eldest brother Robert. Edmund pushed his lips together but couldn't stop the slight shake of his head.

'Richard!' Mary opened her arms to him as he walked across the yard.

'I'm sorry I wasn't here.' He kissed her face as she threw her veil back. 'I have been to the grave. It is almost full now,' he intoned. Everyone heard it and Eliza noticed the smiles vanish again.

'You found it?' Henry asked. 'One of the first in the new cemetery.'

Richard nodded. 'A gardener saw me and pointed the way through the gate.'

'I'm so glad that you're here,' said Mary. She looked around the yard. 'This would be a good time,' she said to Robert.

He turned towards his brothers and sisters. 'Mr Totsfield will read the will tomorrow at ten.' He paused and turned to Henry. 'Father expressed a wish to Mr Totsfield that you should be there also.'

Edmund put his plate down so forcefully that it broke in two. 'The yard is mine,' he shouted before striding towards the cottage. Mary called after him but he went inside, banging the door behind him. Robert was by his mother's side a moment later; she cried.

Eliza did not understand what had been said and what was happening but she knew that Aunty Mary was unhappy. Although none of the other adults moved Eliza went to her. Her mother, Mary-Ann, noticed and went to stop her but she wasn't quick enough. Eliza reached up and held Mary's hand.

'I'm sorry that we won't see Uncle Robert again,' she said in a clear voice. No-one moved and the yard was quiet as she continued, 'I liked him. He was a nice man.' Several people in the room smiled. Mary let go of her son and leant down to the young girl and kissed her cheek. Eliza stroked away the tears that were running down Mary's face as empathic tears formed in her own eyes.

Mary stood up and looked at Henry and Mary-Ann who had now moved to stand behind their small daughter. 'She's as special as her father,' Mary stated with a weak smile.

The following morning Henry was in Boulter's the bakers. It was only a quarter to ten and he had arrived early. From the shop he could see the entrance to the yard and he was waiting for others of his cousins to arrive so that he didn't have to enter the cottage on his own. He didn't want a confrontation with Edmund. As he waited he chewed on a small bread roll: he had not felt like eating before he left his house but now the smell of the bakery had awakened his hunger. The shop was busy which meant that Mr Boulter didn't have time to come and ask after Louisa for which Henry was thankful. A few minutes before ten he saw Robert and Richard approaching together and left the shop. Henry was pleased because they seemed happy to see him: he had wondered if they would feel that he was intruding. He knew there would be problems with Edmund that morning and hoped it would not be too unpleasant so the fact that there didn't seem to be hostility from Edmund's brothers made Henry feel easier.

The three men smiled momentarily at each other before entering the yard and walking through to the cottage. Inside they found Mary sat at the table with her three daughters. Edmund could be heard walking about upstairs. Robert and Richard each went up to their mother and kissed her. Henry hung back but Mary smiled at him.

'And you as well Henry,' she said. Unhesitatingly he went to her. 'I know this is going to be difficult,' she continued, 'but I'm so grateful. Robert was a lot easier in his mind the last few years.'

'We'll have to see how it works out,' replied Henry, 'but I'll do my best.' At that moment Edmund blundered into the room and then stopped when he saw Henry and his mother. He turned to his brothers, with his back to Henry.

'I'm sure I don't know why father asked for Henry to be here,' he said loudly. Henry and Mary looked at each other but said nothing.

'We'll find out soon enough,' suggested Robert. 'I know father thought very highly of Henry.'

Just then the bell to the yard rang and Robert went out to bring Mr Totsfield through to the cottage. When all the men and Mary sat down round the table Henry found himself opposite Edmund who was on one side of Mary with Robert on the other. Edmund stared at Henry malevolently. The will was read and during the reading Edmund gradually lost his frown as it appeared that his father had not left the yard to Henry. But he was puzzled: *why did he especially ask for Henry to be there?* He watched his mother smile weakly at Henry. *That's it – father thought that perhaps Robert and Richard wouldn't be here and that Henry could support mother. Well that's great. I'm sure he enjoyed hearing the will read.*

Mr Totsfield cleared his throat. 'There is a codicil to this will.' The room went quiet and Edmund's frown returned. He did not say anything while the codicil was read; he remained quiet whilst it was explained; he was unconcerned. So, his mother had to agree to his decisions about the yard: what did she know? He was her son and even as a young child he could circumnavigate anything she put in his way. Mr Totsfield left.

'Well I don't know what you hoped for from that,' challenged Edmund. He was not looking at anyone but everyone knew that he was speaking to Henry. Henry did not reply. 'I still have the yard.' Henry remained silent but looked at Robert and Richard. 'I have the yard.' Edmund repeated, his voice raised.

'Yes, Edmund, the yard is yours,' Mary stated quietly, 'but you will not make any decisions without asking me first.'

'I don't understand.' Edmund looked wildly about the room. 'You don't know anything about running the yard.'

'No Edmund, mother doesn't,' Robert cut through Edmund's panic, 'however, Henry does. Don't you see? That's why Henry is here. Father made him her advisor whilst he was still alive.'

At this Edmund laughed, short, high-pitched and harsh, the evidence of malice not mirth. 'I'm mother's son. She'll do what I want. She won't listen to –'

'But I will,' Mary interrupted him but then paused. 'I will listen to Henry because I have sworn to follow his advice. Your father wanted me to do it. In spite of all the training he gave you he did not think that you could run the yard.'

Edmund glared round the room and then strode over to the door that led upstairs. He turned to face Henry.

'You run it. You run the yard. But it's my name over the door and it belongs to me. You'll work it but your children won't inherit it. It's mine.' He went upstairs and the door banged behind him.

Printed in Poland
by Amazon Fulfillment
Poland Sp. z o.o., Wrocław